I0784854

Seeking Reality
A Collection of Metaphysical Short Stories

by Dennis Wammack, (c)2025 a251102
All rights are reserved.

Paperback: ISBN 978-1-965619-16-2
eBook: ISBN-978-1-965619-17-9

For rights and permissions, contact Dennis Wammack, denniswammack@gmail.com. denniswammack.com

Cover design by the author using artificial intelligence resources. Published by DCW Press, Birmingham, Alabama, dcwpress.com.

Author's Note

This collection of short stories begins at the end and ends at the beginning. The first story is the culmination of my attempt to make sense of everything: "What's it all about? Why? That kind of thing. The last is the beginning of my writing career, when I first began to translate thought into communication. The stories in between are random metaphysical stories, usually whimsical, sometimes absurd, exploring the implications of quantum physics on the nature of the universe and our concepts of reality.

I don't claim to be right. Just more right than others.

This book is dedicated to my parents, their celebration of life, and all who join them.

Peace.

Dennis Wammack

~~~~~~

God is the lion that eats the wildebeest.

Ripping its still-living body,
consuming its still-living flesh.

Without mercy,
without compassion,
without guilt.

God is the Wildebeest.

~~~~~~

TABLE OF CONTENTS

Six.
Scratching Schrodinger's Cat

By Dennis Wammack (c)2024. Published in the Hoover Library Write Club 2024 anthology, "Write Club: An Unexpected Journey," ISBN 979-8-227-90263-4, March 2025. Digital format ISBN 978-1-965619-12-4. Published in digital format April 2025 on Draft2Digital. This is the 1048 word revised metaphysical flash fiction version a251102.

Seven.
Dorothy and
The Quantum Mechanic

By Dennis Wammack (c)2014. Published in digital format on Smashwords, May 2014. Published in the paperback anthology, "Seeking Truth, Seeking Why," by Dennis Wammack (c)2020, ISBN 978-0-463306668, published by DCW Press, March 2020. Published in digital format March 2025 on Draft2Digital. This is the 2760 word revised White Light short story version a251102.

Eight.
Country Light

By Dennis Wammack (c)2014. Published in digital format on Smashwords, March 2014. Published in the paperback anthology, "Seeking Truth, Seeking Why," by Dennis Wammack (c)2020, ISBN 978-0-463306668 published by DCW Press March 2020. Published in digital format December 2024 on Draft2Digital. This is the 3550 word revised White Light short story version a251102.

Nine.
Empty Glass

By Dennis Wammack (c)2019. Published in digital format on Smashwords, December 2018. Published in the paperback anthology, "Seeking Truth, Seeking Why," by Dennis Wammack (c)2020, ISBN 978-0-463306668, published by DCW, Press March 2020. Published in digital format March 2020 on Draft2Digital. This is the 3189 word revised short story version a251102.

Ten.
The Compendium
of Reality

The Compendium is my attempt to correct and unify metaphysical terms and concepts explored in these anthologies and to provide some scientific framework for their evolution.

###

ONE

On "Old-Time Religion" and a Modern Concept of God

by Dennis Wammack (c) 2025

The Emergence of Religions

Is religion the world's oldest science?

Early hominids were surely concerned with what caused storms. Perhaps they reasoned that storms were caused by a powerful force living in the sky, and this hypothesis evolved into Zeus, Yahweh, and other storm deities. Scholars may know, but I don't, how the Greeks simultaneously laid the foundation for the Scientific Method while formalizing the Olympian pantheon of gods. Had religion been a true science, the concept of gods controlling nature would have been replaced as scholars discovered natural causes.

But then, religion also provides a deep connection among humans.

This became more important as agriculture developed and cities grew. The size of hunter-gatherer tribes was limited to around 200 members—the approximate limit where the tribal chief and members could know every other member: who to trust, who to rely on, who to fear. In large cities, people were no longer interconnected by tribal membership, but belief in a common god provided a framework wherein members could "belong to the same tribe."

Gods and goddesses were abundant in ancient civilizations and existed mostly in harmony. Ancient Canaanite writers, however, changed this narrative. Emerging from their writings of three thousand years ago were new, and in my mind, several harmful concepts. Three major "old-time-religions" emerged that incorporated these concepts—the Abrahamic religions of Judaism, Christianity, and Islam.

It is my religious belief than science is the unfolding word of God. If this belief is valid, then I believe religions should reconsider their stance when confronted with conflicting accepted science. To encourage a progressive and inclusive future for humankind, all religions, especially the Abrahamic religions, should renegotiate these three fundamental concepts through the lens of three thousand years of God's revelations.

The First Concept:
"Our writings are the inerrant word of God and cannot be changed."

When subjected to the Scientific Method, this concept is indefensible by definition. If you hold this to be true, I urge you to renegotiate the concept.

The Second Concept:
"My god is the only God, and all other gods are false gods,"
with its all too often corollary,
"You may righteously kill nonbelievers, if it suits your purpose."

Not true? Just ask an ultra-conservative member of any Abrahamic religion. Hence, John Lennon's somewhat cynical song "Imagine."

The Third Concept:
"The female is subordinate to the male."

Ah. Here we have it; perhaps the most dehumanizing of the three; a devourer of hope and humanity. This horse gallops across a bloody crimson sky, carrying self-righteous men, cloaked in the armor of their god, trampling uppity women (and anyone else who opposes them). Think Afghanistan, Iran, ISIS. Think of any country where a woman fears to walk unveiled.

But this concept is far more insidious than those extremes. It permeates and weakens Western civilization. Wherever there is an Abrahamic religion, women are routinely subjugated. Misogyny is integral to their culture.

Which is interesting, because before the influence of the early Canaanite writers, for every god, there was a goddess—a consort, wife, concubine, sister, or mother. But the Canaanite writers killed off all the goddesses; specifically, Asherah, who happened to be Yahweh's wife and a powerful, highly regarded goddess in her own right. But Asherah, Lilith, and the other powerful females did not fit into the Canaanite concept of patriarchy. They had to go.

Rather than "They created Male and Female in their likeness," consider "They created Masculinity and Femininity in their likeness." Masculinity/Femininity is a better fit with Platonic "Essences," Eastern Yin/Yang, and non-gendered gods. More importantly, the word "Femininity" carries the concept of "One who gives birth and nurtures." Masculinity carries the concept of "One who protects and provides."

And who better to lead a church than "One who nurtures." This would place the woman in the leadership position and men in the "support and provide" role. Hence, if Asherah and Mary Magdalene had not been canceled, the Catholic Church might require a feminine Pope and Bishops supported by masculine Cardinals and Priests.

The ancient Egyptian concept of "Ma'at" requires balance in all things. Especially in male-female relationships that have been, in my opinion, stressed with twenty-five hundred years of misogyny, leaving our social, religious, political, and business systems under complete control of the often toxic "Masculine" without sufficient influence and guidance from the "Feminine." The two are designed to complement one another with co-equal dependencies and strengths ... to maintain Ma'at. One without the other devolves into the Western civilization we have today.

Beyond Old-Time Religions

Each person's relationship with their god and their religion is limited by their knowledge and experience. They cannot relate to, nor understand, a god outside these limitations. Otherwise, every religious belief is valid for the believer and needs no defense. Religious beliefs, as long as they do no harm, strengthen the individual, promote community and good works, fulfill the basic need to belong, and interact with our "Awareness of God." Any one of these functions would validate their religion. It is the believer's best effort to know an unknowable God.

Still, major world religions are based on writings over two thousand years old, and have not adjusted to two thousand years of the unfolding word of God.

My goal is not to dismiss anyone's religious beliefs but rather to posit a modern concept of God more consistent with current scientific thought.

A Modern God

My concept of a modern god is a variation of pantheism, a philosophy first proposed by Baruch Spinoza in the 1660s, developed using the deductive reasoning method. My conclusion, however, developed independently while writing *Metaphysics 101: Insemination, Gestation, Birth, and Evolution of Viable Universes,* which explored the impossibilities of quantum mechanics from a fiction writer's perspective.

Merging quantum dichotomies with a pantheistic universe suggests that all things end at the beginning—Alpha and Omega—at the birth of the Tree of Life—with God.

Today, it is accepted science that humans do not see "Fundamental Reality" but see only the reality necessary for us to survive and procreate—our "Perceived Reality."

Granting that most religious writers were sincere and inspired by their "Awareness of God," their words were surely filtered through political, economic, and limited understanding of a limitless God. They did their best and got a lot right, but this was over two thousand years ago.

Science requires change. "Give Me That Old-Time Religion," "Vaccines are Unproven," and "Alternate Truths" are all fear and rejection of change. Our kind does not like change. Change is hard. Change may rip us from a community in which we are loved, accepted, and understood—where we *are* somebody!

"Give Me That Old-Time Religion" is a plea for "Don't make me change!" Anyone reading this far is searching and changing.

The searches for religion, self, meaning, and God are different journeys. For the first, I suggest finding a religion and congregation where the members share your worldview and sensibilities. The details don't matter that much. Eastern religions and philosophies are probably a good place to search for "self."

But if you search for the meaning of life or the nature of God, then consider what follows.

My God

The following statements are deductions developed in my short story, *The Answer: A Scientific Fantasy on Themes by Zarathustra, Spinoza, and Planck.*

"Consciousness" is a fundamental property of the vibrating strings that compose the universe.

"Time" is an emergent property of the interaction between vibrating strings and exists only at such interaction.

"Experience" is the record of each such interaction.

"The Tree of Life" is composed of all vibrating strings created by the Big Bang and is the body of God.

All strings are entangled with every other string. The aggregate of their Experiences generated over time is the Consciousness of God.

Since all vibrating strings are connected to every other string, then all things are connected and, with varying degrees, are aware of each other.

The experience of a sunrise on a crisp morning, the overpowering presence of the sea, lightening in a tumultuous sky followed by the rumble of nature unleashed, a shaft of light falling on green leaves in a forest, a child's laughter— these things may be examples of this awareness, this sense of interconnectedness—a collective consciousness. Perhaps, you are experiencing an existence larger than yourself.

Label the experience whatever you wish, but my label is "Awareness of God."

Awareness

A rock has Consciousness—its Experience of being a rock. It may not have Awareness (or maybe in the world of rocks, it does). But I will posit that Consciousness emerges into the emergent property of Awareness in all living organisms. All living things can respond to outside stimuli, make adjustments, and take action to survive.

The forest knows when a tree has been damaged. The damaged tree releases organic compounds, electrical signals, and popping sounds. Information is shared with other trees through underground fungal networks. A flower communicates to a bee that another bee has recently taken the flower's pollen by a change in its magnetic field. If you are aware of the flower, perhaps the flower is aware of you. You, being higher on the evolutionary scale, are more aware than the flower is—but then, who am I to say? Awareness does not require intelligence, just as intelligence does not require deductive reasoning.

Reasoning

As "Awareness" is an emergent property of living material, "Reasoning" is an emergent property of highly evolved living material. Historically thought to be the sole domain of human beings, science continues to extend the capacity to reason to other species. Not only do elephants, wolves, and crows recognize their dead, but it's probable they also mourn their dead. Bonobos and chimps are now being observed developing a spoken language. Their grunts, screams, and calls carry different meanings depending on the order of their vocalizations.

I don't wish to anthropomorphize rocks, plants, or animals, but rather suggest that humans are nothing more than low fruit on the universally interconnected Tree of Life.

The One—The All

The Big Bang was the birth of God—its body, the Tree of Life— its consciousness, a blank slate.

God's consciousness evolves with the acquisition of ever-evolving Consciousness. This acquisition takes place when an entity ceases to exist through destruction or death. The entity is no longer subject to the influence of time, and its Experience is incorporated into Fundamental Reality. God gains Experience when it acquires yours.

This, then, is your purpose—to gather Experience for the Universe to grow and evolve.

You die, but the Consciousness that gave you Awareness continues. At the moment of death, your Experience is incorporated into the Experience of God. Since all things are interconnected, you have access to the totality of God's Experience, which is everything that has ever happened. There is no time. You experience all things.

The details may be poorly conceptualized, but I hold that my concept is closer to truth than Abraham's.

So, the next time you are struck with a moment of unbearable beauty, peace, or awe—savor it ... glory in it... embrace it ... give yourself to it. If my concept is viable, you may be experiencing awareness of Alpha and Omega ... of all who preceded you ... of all that's ever been ... of the living, evolving, conscious, self-aware Universe ... of God.

###

~~~~~~~~~~~~~~~~~~~~~~~~~~~~~~~~

TWO

~~~~~~~~~~~~~~~~~~~~~~~~~~~~~~~~

The Field Where God Was Born

by Dennis Wammack (c) 2025

Two scientists and a mathematician get together in the canteen to discuss their quantum physics research. Elsewhere, Foxie and Teumessian reprise their roles as tavern keepers. They help God (pronouns: they/them) find what they didn't know they were searching for.

Two stories, different worlds, ending in the same place—at the beginning.

The Field #1

Three world-leading, Nobel Laureate experts sat in the Planck Deep Lab canteen doing what they do best: arguing about data interpretation. Mannlich and Donna were at each other's throats. Suri listened to them babble.

Dr. Albert Mannlich argued in his thick, German accent, "I'm within three orders of magnitude of achieving life-size magnification of the Planck field. I see absolutely no suggestion of Loop Gravity!"

Dr. Sophia Donna replied in her sweet Berkeley-ized Italian accent, "Nor, dummkopf, preclude it!"

They fussed on for a while. Donna finally said, "You have been quiet, Sats. Do you want to weigh in on his latest results?"

Dr. Satyendra Suri's Indian, Oxford-educated response, to some degree, calmed the conversation. He said, "The mathematical results appear to be indisputable, but I wonder if the visual presentation is masking pertinent underlying progressions. Your selection of false colors is arbitrary. The colors emphasize areas containing probable electromagnetic variations but may be deemphasizing areas of commonality. I can write a plug-in for your next run to allow you to vary false colors in real-time. Maybe different combinations will yield insight into how to interpret the data."

Mannlich responded, with less agitation, "I'm not going to waste time coloring my optical Planck field maps with pretty colors!"

Sats suggested, "Transfer enough funds to cover my costs, and I can train an AI to analyze different color combinations across different intensity levels with differing smoothing algorithms. I can have it return the most promising color maps."

Sophie interjected, "I'll fund some of that project if you can represent my multi-dimensional gravitational data on a piece of paper."

"I can do better. I can display your curves utilizing interactive holograms."

Mannlich, seeing his colleague possibly pulling ahead in her research, hastily added, "Very well. I will cover half the funding! But only to see Sophie's curves undulating in an interactive hologram."

Sophie shouted to the room, "HR! HR!! Where in god's name is HR when a girl needs them?!"

Where God Was Born #1

Once upon a time, in a world not too far away, God was walking through a shimmering forest and came upon a quaint tavern. They decided to enter, walked through the door, and took a seat at the end of the bar.

On the other side of the bar stood an attractive vixen. She asked, "What'll y'all have, Mamsir?"

God considered and replied with their manly voice, "I'll have whatever your random number generator comes up with," then added with their softer, more feminine voice, "But apply Occam's Razor, please."

The fox replied, "You got it! A double Aqua coming right up!"

God commanded, "Add a double whiskey to that," then softly added, "On the rocks with a squeezed lemon wedge and maybe a little sweetener, please. But not too sweet."

Foxie politely hesitated, waiting for maybe more instructions, then beamed, and again replied, "Double Old Fashion comin' right up!"

God surveyed their domain. At the far end of the bar, a monkey sat furiously typing away on a laptop. In the darkened corner sat an imposing fox staring intently into nothingness.

As Foxie delivered the double Old Fashion and a bowl of warm mixed nuts, God said, "Nice place you got here," then added, "Very warm and inviting."

"Thank you, Mamsir. The most interesting people in our world find their way here. I love it!"

"I would think you would be bored—out in the woods—a monkey and whoever that is in the corner are your only customers," then added, "Yet charming and peaceful."

Foxie was not miffed. She simply glanced at the monkey and said, "Monkey, write a story about it raining hard in here."

The monkey typed away. Suddenly, a dark cloud formed in the ceiling, a streak of lightning flashed from the clouds to the cash register with a boom, and a torrential rain began falling inside the tavern.

Foxie admired Monkey's handiwork and said, "That's enough, Monkey. Make it stop and dry us off."

Monkey typed. The rain stopped. The ceiling glowed with warming heat, the humidity dropped, a gentle drying breeze blew, and the room—with everyone in it—soon returned to normal.

Foxie looked at God and smiled a little Mona Lisa fox smile.

God thundered, "Hell! I can't even do that!" Then softly added, "I feel like I just left the spa. This is wonderful!"

Foxie replied, "This isn't *your* story. You have the stage, but you must play your part just like everybody else."

"I thought this *was* my story. Everybody has got to do what I want them to do," then added, "For their own good, of course."

Foxie said, "Oh, my God. You're so sweet!"

The Field #2

Sats stood staring lovingly at his quantum computer, overwhelmed with wonder, respect, and joy. *Unknowable Brahman ... All things ... Do I stand before new knowledge ... if it is there, let me be worthy to receive it.*

Numbers ... sequences ... concepts continuously flowed through his mind as the Ganges flows through Varanasi. Sats' consciousness was now filled with the challenge of the two projects laid before him.

He returned to his workstation, picked up his Chai, and sipped it while considering his instructions on the screen. *This wasn't as simple as I envisioned. Imaging data and gravity measurements simply don't lend themselves to commonality in input OR output. Starting with Sophie's project may anger Manny, but hers is the more complex problem. Displaying more than four dimensions of data is as much art as science. Perhaps more. But Sophie's easy to work with, and Manny appears to be growing fond of her.*

Sats reprimanded himself for improper thought, breathed his mantra, then commanded, "GREAT SARASWATI." He prayed, *Hear my song, apply your wisdom, reveal the meaning.* "EXECUTE!"

The AI, upon being initiated with the term "great saraswati," loaded the instructions into the quantum computer nicknamed "Saraswati" and patiently waited as Saraswati applied her wisdom to Sophie's questions.

As Sats sat sipping his Chai, Sophie and Manny sat in the canteen fussing over gravity loop theory. They sat close together. So they would not have to talk too loudly.

Where God Was Born #2

Finishing their second Old Fashion, the vixen was becoming prettier and prettier. God wondered about the propriety of mating with a fox. God leaned in and asked, "Hey, Babe, what time do you get off?" But quickly added, "You are a very lovely fox."

Foxie laughed as she replied, "Sorry, Mamsir, but I never get off unless it's with my man-friend sitting in the corner. He has the most gorgeous tail in the world! I get the twitchies just thinking about it. I can ring the outside party bell if you want to party with some nice, exciting woodland creatures. The ducks around here can really dance up a storm."

God said, "No. I'll just sit here and enjoy the whiskey." Then added, "And the company, of course."

As Foxie delivered the third Old Fashion, she glanced at the darkened corner table. The imposing fox sitting there nodded as he looked at their customer.

Foxie discreetly acknowledged his instruction, looked at God, and asked, "I haven't seen you around here before. Where you from?"

God replied, "Oh. Nowhere. Everywhere." Then added somewhat sadly, "From wherever I wish to be, I suppose."

"World traveler. That's exciting. Were you born around here?"

"Born? I don't think I was ever born. I've always been around." Then added, "What an insightful question. We sometimes wonder about that."

Foxie offered, "You don't know your roots? Your people? That's so sad. Would you like to commiserate with my husband? His name is Teumessian. He's very wise."

"Yeah. Sure. Why not?" Then added, "That would be delightful."

Foxie looked into the darkened corner and called out, "Toomy, come visit our customer. They don't have a home!"

God glanced at Teumessian and gestured for the fox to join them.

Teumessian rose to his full, impressive height, picked up his Pellegrino, approached the bar, and sat beside God. He said, "Welcome to our Home. I've been eavesdropping on your conversation. 'Nowhere and Everywhere.' That's rather metaphysical, isn't it?"

God was puzzled. "Metaphysical? What does that mean?" Then added, "That sounds deep and complex. I don't *think* I'm metaphysical!"

Toomy held up his glass of Pellegrino in salute. "Wonderful! Then tell me where you were born!"

God thundered, "I was not born! I have always been here!" But quickly added, "Although I did give birth and nurture all of nature, you know!"

Teumessian was not intimidated. He quietly responded, "Yes, yes. You did give birth to all things. Without you, nothing would exist. It appears this topic stirs deep feelings within you. Perhaps one day you'll find out."

God was somewhat mollified. "I never knew my mother. I don't know *where* I was born." Then added, "That's sad, isn't it? It would be rather nice to know."

Toomy sipped his Pellegrino as he gazed into God's eyes. God's fist clenched. God's heart fluttered.

Toomy said, "You were born fourteen billion years ago. Nothing existed until you were born. From you, all things were made. From you, all things came into being. You are all things, and all things are you. The question remains, *where* were you born?"

God looked at the barkeep. "Bring me another drink." Then added, "Please."

Foxie decided to ring the party bell.

The Field #3

A full month had passed since Sats' offer to generate visual interpretations for Sophie and Manny's data sets. Sats had only yesterday generated an acceptable proposal for Sophie's holographic interpretation of quantum Loop data and had only then begun working on Manny's quantum field imaging project. He had made an offering to Vishnu for protection against Manny's potential self-righteous anger.

The presentation would take place in the Lab's holographically equipped conference room. Sats' presentation was prepared specifically for Dr. Donna, although her growing admirer, Dr. Mannlich, was also invited to attend. But word had spread throughout the facility, and the observer seats were almost all occupied by uninvited guests. Few scientists in the Planck Quantum Deep Lab were that interested in Loop Gravity, but still, it would be an interesting presentation, make a good entry for weekly activity reports, and Services provided the very best coffee and doughnuts. One must do one's duty.

Ten a.m. arrived. Dr. Suri mounted the podium, looked out over the visitors, glanced at Dr. Mannlich, nodded to Dr. Donna, closed his eyes, bowed his head, breathed, opened his eyes, and thundered, "Welcome!" He continued on with his standard greetings, followed by an overview of Dr. Donna's data along with a simplified explanation of his methodology in translating her data into a holographic presentation, which he had arbitrarily set to an eleven-minute duration. Although this meeting was solely for the benefit of Dr. Donna, Sats asked her to briefly describe the data that she and the audience would be viewing this morning. She exclaimed that she would be delighted to do so.

Forty-five minutes into the brief presentation, observing a fidgeting audience, Sats rose and suggested a quick break with the holographic presentation to begin in exactly fifteen minutes.

While waiting, Sats apologized to Manny for taking so long on Sophie's side of the project, but assured him that the "lessons learned" would benefit Manny in the long term. Manny was uncharacteristically docile and assured Sats that it was more important that Sophie's data be presented to the limits of Sats' capabilities. Sats thanked Manny. *Thank you, Lord Vishnu!*

The fifteen minutes lapsed, and Dr. Suri escorted Dr. Donna to the primary viewing seat. Dr. Mannlich followed. They sat down. Dr. Suri commanded, "GREAT SARASWATI: Project Suri hologram number one for an eleven-minute duration. EXECUTE!"

The room lights slowly lowered to complete darkness. The hologram appeared. It began.

Of all the attendees, including Sophie and Manny, Sats was the most mesmerized. He left this world and entered a world of pure mathematics, emerging Fibonacci sequences ... physically impossible forms appearing, seguing into other impossible forms, emerging into higher dimensions. To Sophie's annoyance, String Theory's eleventh dimension slowly emerged. Sats' mind had merged with the hologram. The presentation ended. The room was totally dark until the lights began to brighten.

Sophie sat in silence as she considered the implications of what she had just witnessed.

Murmurs of appreciation ran through the audience.
"I want to see *that* again. Munching magic mushrooms."
"I didn't recognize any quantum gravity loops, but I saw everything else."
"Dr. Donna's curves are always interesting."

Sats rose and thanked the audience for their interest. He left Sophie and Manny to their quiet, but intense, conversation. This was Sats' first full, uninterrupted viewing of the presentation. He was unsure of what he had just witnessed. *Goddess Saraswati ... I have witnessed the eleventh dimension and it is beyond my knowing ... open my mind ... reveal to me what my eyes have seen ...*

Where God Was Born #3

The tavern was hopping—literally. Rabbits. Frogs. Birds. Two kangaroos. Ducks were dancing a line dance. A snake was wrapped around the cash register, sizing up a particularly delightful-looking frog. Foxie walked by and snapped, "Behave in here!"

God, on their fifth Old Fashion, was having existential and bladder crises.

Toomy volunteered, "It's out back and to the right. Don't fall into the pool."

God grunted, "Thanks," and added, "I won't be long."

Foxie ambled over to Toomy and asked, "Everything all right?"

Toomy said, "God is enjoying our offerings. It's all we have a right to hope for. So, everything is fine. Unless he falls into the pool."

"God seems conflicted. Like, part wants to know where they were born, but part doesn't. But they share information with you because you care."

"Maybe it's you who should be drinking with them. It's *you* who came up with that fourteen billion years ago insight. I still don't understand where you came up with it."

She laughed. "From a little voice inside my head. That was before you came into my life."

He chuckled. "Maybe I should go away so you can get back to business."

She instinctively grabbed his paw. "No! Don't even joke about that! Without you, I am incomplete."

"We are a good team, Babe. I'm not going anywhere."

God reentered the room. They were covered with printer's ink. They had fallen into the pool.

The Field #4

Manny and Sophie were having lunch in the canteen. They now sat in the far corner away from the main eating area. It was quieter there. A little dark for a business lunch, but it would have to do.

Sophie was excited that Sats was about to complete Manny's "Planck Field Electromagnetic Distribution" hologram.

Manny was saying, "I don't expect it to be as dramatic as yours, Sophie. I can only record a two-dimensional slice at a time. I expect it to be a static display, but if he can smooth out the variations, it might be helpful in the long term. I need another full order of magnitude increase in resolution before I can even begin to conceptualize how a visual interpretation of a Planck field would appear. If I can ever achieve it, I will be staring into the face of god himself!"

She giggled. "Or into the field where she was born."

"Yes, yes. But we should not anthropomorphize god."

"And if we do—god's a she, not a he!"

"If I photograph a penis and testicles, then god is a he!"

"Get over it! Men are just jealous!"

Sophie was interrupted as Sats came up and asked if he could join them.

Manny half-rose as he answered, "Yes, yes, of course. What news?"

"Good and bad. The hologram is not static. It's a cacophony of shifting unrelated colors. But I find this interesting: the colors don't appear to be arbitrary. No matter how many times I command Saraswati to apply false colors to ambiguous data, she returns the same set of colors. To her, the data are not ambiguous. Explain *that*."

"At a thousand-to-one resolution, *all* data are approximations. There's no way that all of the data is unambiguous!"

Sophie sat listening. When the two men came to a lull, she offered, "Well, Saraswati believes all the data to be realistic. Ask her to connect the color values into a multidimensional shape where there is no disconnect between each value. Maybe we will get a nice multi-dimensional abstract suitable for framing."

Sats exclaimed, "Of course! Let Goddess Saraswati reveal to us what we are seeing!"

Manny set down his cup of coffee—hard. "Schwachsinn! This holographic project is hopeless. I need a double whiskey!"

Where God Was Born #4

Dawn would soon arrive. The party was winding down. The woodland creatures were hopping, flying, and dragging themselves into their tomorrow. An excited snake had left early and curled up at a nice, secluded spot next to the pathway. A general alert filtered through the frog community. God, still covered with printer's ink, sat with their head lying on the bar.

Foxie and Toomy watched the "resting" god as she washed glasses and Toomy bussed the tables.

She said, "I told Monkey to take God outside and clean them up as soon as the sun rises."

"God's a mess, all right. Printer's ink from head to toe. I don't know why you keep that stuff around."

Monkey wants me to keep the pool full for whenever laptops disappear. He will need the ink to write his stories. Monkey says that when a thing which is not known is covered with ink, when you remove the excess ink, what remains is the truth of the thing. I don't know what he's talking about, but he can make it rain whenever he wants to."

Toomy murmured, "Let's go to the patio and watch the sun rise. Monkey can send God out to get cleaned whenever they wake up."

She joined Toomy, and they walked onto the patio; his arm around her shoulder, her arm around his waist. They walked to the patio edge to where the infinite field began. Soft light was bringing morning to the quaint tavern in the shimmering forest somewhere in a world not too far away.

The Field #5

Dr. Mannlich's phone was insistent. It was three in the morning. He finally picked up and grogged, "Yes?"

The voice on the other end was uncharacteristically demanding, "Manny, Manny. Come to the Holo Room! Now!"

"Sats, are you all right? What's happening?"

Sats demanded, "Manny! Come now!" and hung up.

Manny sighed and poked the body lying next to him.

The body muttered, "Again, cowboy?! You're insatiable! All right. One more time!"

Manny said, "It's Sats. He wants me to come to the Holo Room immediately."

Sophie said, "It's God o'clock in the morning, Manny. Can't he wait?"

"He was insistent, Sophie ... and excited."

"All right, but I'm going with you."

They dressed and called for transportation from the residences to the main lab facilities. On the way, Manny kept wondering what could possibly be so important. Sophie snuggled against his arm and sleepily ignored his blathering.

They arrived at the labs, passed through security, and walked to the Holo projection room. Sats was there, staring into the hologram.

Sats looked utterly exhausted. He began without preamble, "I did what you suggested, but your data still didn't make sense any way I projected it. Finally, I changed the data set from a two-dimensional 1000 by 1000 slice to a three-dimensional 1000 by 1000 by 1000 slice. The false colors began trying to make patterns. In exasperation, I told Saraswati to optimize the dimensions of the data set to optimize continuity of the data. It took her three hours, but she did it. By the way, Saraswati believes the exact dimensions of your field of view are 1242 by 1238 by 811 Planck units, a color is assigned to each Planck volume, and she can generate a hologram for user-defined colors. The holograms appear to be collections of various numeric sequences."

Manny was growing agitated, "That's not the results I was expecting. How confident are you that you're not just tweaking algorithms to generate results you want? I want a visual image of the field, not some mathematical representation. But I see why you are so excited. Maybe I can use this information in some way."

Sats stared blankly at Manny. "I generated this information three days ago. This is a routine investigation. This isn't exciting! This isn't exciting at all!"

Where God Was Born #5

In a different story, in a different world, two foxes stand, anthropomorphically arm in arm, looking at a sunrise over a shimmering field of vibrant colors. A gentle rain is beginning, soon to wash away the black ink covering an Old-Fashion infused, enigmatic, powerful, melancholy guest. The foxes were patient.

The ink-covered God eventually walked past the two foxes into the gentle rain and stood with outstretched arms as the rain washed away the blackness covering them. God stared over the shimmering, ever-changing, endless field of wildflowers. Colors growing in vibrant and subtle rows and shapes. A field alive with endless swaying shapes—interconnected—giving greater meaning and life to one another. A field of endless, living shapes, given birth by the endless field—nurturing—awash with meaning— yielding beauty and variation without end—a field without end.

Baptized by the rain, uncertainty washed away, God stared mesmerized at the living field. The sun appeared and dried the cleansed world.

God walked deep into the field, fell to their knees, placed their head upon the ground, and whispered, "Mother, we are home."

The Field #6

Sats continued, more excitedly, "No, no, no! What happened is that Fibonacci sequences began emerging, then Topology forms emerged. Then I commanded Saraswati to correlate your data with Sophie's. She computed a correlation of point seven. That's when I became excited. I told her to propagate the dataset back in time as far as she could. It required her resources for almost a full day, but the apparent result is staggering." He commanded, "GREAT

SARASWATI: Project Donna-Mannlich Hologram Run Number Eleven, frame by frame, beginning with the first empty frame. EXECUTE!"

The hologram began. It projected no information. Only the Power-On light indicated it was displaying data. Sats offered, "You two are the quantum physicists. I can only postulate that there *is* no Planck field in this frame. He commanded, "GREAT SARASWATI: Advance one frame! EXECUTE!"

The projector advanced the hologram one frame. It projected only maximized brilliant white light. "This frame may suggest that a Singularity has occurred, creating and occupying physical space that did not exist in the last frame. He commanded, "GREAT SARASWATI: Advance one frame! EXECUTE!"

The hologram projected its lowest possible color value to create a solid mass of motionless, repeating purple spheres of Planck volumes. "The Singularity appears to have spontaneously redistributed itself into its smallest parts. A separate Planck volume for each quantum string, perhaps." Sats paused for the two scientists to absorb what he had just suggested, and then quietly said, "Now, it begins." He commanded, "GREAT SARASWATI: Increase display time by a factor of ten every ten seconds. EXECUTE!"

The Planck volumes began to self-organize into straight lines. A few began changing color. The lines and colors began evolving faster. And faster. Shapes began appearing. Dimensions began appearing. More sequences. Endless sequences. Shapes. Endless shapes. A field of endless everything. Volumes rearranging themselves into the most efficient curves.

Manny and Sophie stared at the hologram with fascination. Finally, Sophie looked at Sats and asked, "But Suri, what does this mean? What are we looking at?"

Dr. Satyendra Suri, heir to countless mathematicians who preceded him, quietly answered, "Can you not see it, Sophie? It is so simple now that I see it. Every color represents a Planck volume in Manny's data set and is equivalent to the gravitational value in your data set. They are one and the same. Space reorganizes itself as a function of the evolving values of its interacting Planck volumes.

Numbers are *not* an abstract construct of the human mind. Numbers are physical Planck volumes created at the Big Bang to hold the contents of the deconstructed Singularity. The universe—fundamental reality—is nothing but the physical manifestation of numbers!"

The three stared at the increasingly swift, increasingly complex holographic projection with growing awe and understanding.

Suri whispered, "We are witnessing the birth of God."

THREE

METAPHYSICS 101
Insemination, Gestation, Birth, and Evolution of Viable Universes

by Dennis Wammack (c) 2024

Section I. Labels

Reality, as we perceive it, is incomplete and is not a fundamental property of the universe. It evolved from, and is limited to, our subjective experiences necessary for survival. This *Perceived Reality* is emergent from *Experience* interacting with the phenomena of Biology. Biology is emergent from Chemistry, which is emergent from Physics, which is emergent from the interaction between one-dimensional *Strings* and *Time*.

The previous explanations are accepted scientific concepts. What follows is novel.

~~~

I propose three levels of reality. *Perceived Reality*, which resides at the Newtonian Level, *Transitional Reality*, which resides at the *Quantum Level*, and *Fundamental Reality*.

The following phenomena exist in *Fundamental Reality*.

The *Mathematical Construct* is the omnipresent, spaceless, timeless holding construct defining abstract Mathematics. It is independent of the existence of any Universe and is consistent across all Universes.

A *Singularity* is the transfer of an infinite quantity in one instance of the *Mathematical Construct* into a new instance of the *Mathematical Construct* wherein the infinite quantity is redistributed and converted to non-infinite quantities.

Seed is my label for the product of a *Singularity*.
~~~

Time-Zero is the instance of a *Seed* being delivered into a newly emergent *Space*. This is a misnomer because *Time* and *Space* have yet to emerge.

~~~

Universe is the resulting product of a viable *Seed* and exists at all three levels of reality.

~~~

The following phenomena emerge from *Fundamental Reality* and exist at the *Quantum Level*.

Space is an emergent property from the interaction between the *Mathematics Construct* and a *Singularity*. It is necessary for the *Mathematical Construct* to receive the *Seed* produced and transferred by the *Singularity*.

Strings are the components of a *Seed* after the *Seed* is delivered into a *Space*.

Time is an emergent property from the interaction between *Strings*.

Experience is imprinted on a *String* as the *String* interacts with other *Strings*. *Strings* had no *Experience* at *Time-Zero*.

Consciousness is the aggregate *Experience* of a *String*.

Collective-Consciousness is the aggregate *Experience* of all *Strings* composing a *Universe*.

Inextricable-Entanglement is the non-emergent condition of the separable contents of a *Seed* being inextricably connected.

Entanglement is the emergent property of *Strings* being linked when spatially separated.

Gravity is the attraction of a spatially separated *String* to all other *Strings* seeking the elimination of the spatial separation.

Section II. Insemination, Gestation, Birth

Our *Mother Universe* was much like our universe. As such, she could create Black Holes which might, or might not, give birth to a new universe such as ours.

The birthing process is similar across all universes. It is this.

Matter gathers. Stars form. Some stars become so dense that they collapse into Black Holes. Black Holes capture more passing matter. Upon entering the Black Hole, the information from the captured matter is stripped away at the Black Hole's Event Horizon, but the *Strings* carrying the information continue to the center of the black hole. The Black Hole becomes more massive because the associated information is retained by the Event Horizon.

Emergent Properties of a *Universe* are not applicable inside a Black Hole. These include the original Emergent Properties such as *Space, Gravity, Time*, and *Entropy*, plus all other Emergent Properties of the *Mother Universe*.

If sufficient mass is gathered so that the mass of the Black Hole will become infinite, then a *Singularity* occurs.

Since Infinity is not allowed in the omnipresent *Mathematical Construct*, that which causes an infinite phenomenon must be relocated outside the *Mother Universe* into a heretofore undefined *Space*. This relocation is the function of the *Singularity*. In this explanation, the *Seed* inside the *Singularity* is formed because of the approaching infinite mass of the Black Hole. The *Singularity* ejects the *Seed* from the *Mother Universe*. The Event Horizon of the *Mother Universe* is not part of the Seed and is therefore not transmitted.

Within the *Singularity*, the *Seed* has no information or Emergent Properties. The *Seed* is now only infinite *Strings* that are infinitely small and require no *Space* because *Space* has yet to emerge. This is *Time-Zero* of our Universe.

Since the *Mathematical Construct* cannot contain any structure that is infinitely small, the interaction between the *Mathematical Construct* and the *Singularity* causes the phenomena of *Space* to emerge in order to hold the *Seed*. This interaction deconstructs the *Singularity* by redistributing the contents of the *Seed* into, in this case, individual *Strings* vibrating with high Compression Energy.

All newly created *Strings* are maximally *Entangled*. *Entanglement* exists in *Space* because *Space* has emerged, but it exists independently of *Time* and *Gravity* since neither has yet emerged.

At Singularity Deconstruction, the compression energy of the *Strings* creates an evaporation event whereby the *Strings* boil into a collection of quantum foam. *Space* expands concurrently with the *Strings* separating into the Foam.

Two *Strings* collide. They interact. Depending on the frequency of each *String*, this interaction will produce a new configuration. These interactions occur independently of *Time* because *Time* has yet to emerge. The interaction between these *Strings* can result in many potential configurations. We label this interaction and potential as a *Quantum Wave Function*. Upon the wave's collapse, a new configuration exists. The ending configuration is different from the beginning configuration. *Time* emerges between the collapse and the reformation of the wave function. The *Strings* are permanently imprinted with the ending configuration information. I label this information bit *Experience* and the aggregate *Experience* bits of the string as *Consciousness*.

All *Strings* are bound to all other *Strings* because of *Inextricable-Entanglement*. We label this attraction *Gravity*. The strength of the attraction is the function of *Space*, *Time*, and *Aggregate Consciousness*. The equation quantifying this attraction has yet to be derived.

Fundamental Reality of the *Mathematical Construct* and the *Seed* have now expanded to include *Space, Entanglement, Time, Experience, Gravity,* and *Consciousness*.

A *Universe* has now been born. It is ready to evolve.

A new *Universe* evolves based on the values of nineteen physical Universal Constants. Most births are short-lived because variation from the optimum in any one of these values will restrict expansion, and the universe can no longer evolve. Our Universal Constants are identical to our mothers. We continue to exist.

The common label for the birth of our universe is *The Big Bang*. A more appropriate label would be *The Birth of the Tree of Life*.

Section III. Evolution of Our Universe

We were born 13.8 billion years ago.

From our explosive birth, all that was and is began to grow and expand. The Tree of Life grew as it created quanta of energy, of light, of matter. Eventually, this great trunk grew into interstellar dust, and galaxies formed. Within galaxies, solar systems formed. And planets and moons. On planets that contained water, life formed. If conditions allowed, life became ever increasingly complex, leading to intelligence. Regardless of intelligence, however, all matter is interconnected, simply different parts of the metaphorical Tree.

Our local limb is our sun and all that our sun influences and produces. The Earth is but one of our sun's children. Earth has produced abundant and varied life, different types, and many species. All life on Earth is interconnected. Each member of a species is simply a different leaf on the same twig.

Given that every string emerging from the *Seed* is *Entangled*, then the *Universe* emerged from the *Seed*. Using the analogy of The Tree of Life as the *Universe*, then the Tree of Life is the body of the *Universe*, and *Aggregate Consciousness* is the mind of the *Universe*.

IV. Implications

Additional labels are required to discuss the implications.

Entity is a collection of *Strings* that form a quantifiable structure. It has an identifiable moment of creation and an identifiable moment of extinction. An *Entity* may be living or non-living, cognizant or not cognizant.

Strings gain *Experience* by interacting with other *Strings*. The aggregate *Experience* of a String has been labeled *Consciousness*. I now label the *Aggregate Consciousness* of an *Entity* to be its *Soul*.

Given that all *Strings* are *Inextricably Entangled* at Time-Zero and given that *Time* is an emergent property and does not influence lower-level states, then all *Strings* must exist at Time-Zero imprinted with all *Experiences* which are shared by all other *Strings*. I label this state *Fundamental Reality*.

If an *Entity* is experiencing *Time*, it can only experience *Perceived Reality*. *Time* masks an *Entity's* perception of *Fundamental Reality*. Upon death, the entity no longer passes through *Time* and exists beneath the quantum level. Its perception of *Fundamental Reality* is no longer masked. Death is not the termination of an *Entity's Consciousness* but rather the unmasking of the *Entity's* aggregate *Souls* to *Fundamental Reality*.

Restating this from the reader-centric viewpoint, you will die, you will no longer experience *Time*, your *Consciousness* will exist only below the quantum level, and you will recognize *Fundamental Reality*. Within *Fundamental Reality*, everything that has ever existed still exists. Your *Consciousness* will experience everything in your *Universe* that has ever been experienced.

Without end.

###

FOUR

THE ANSWER REDUX
To Be or Not to Be

by Dennis Wammack, (c) 2024

"What existed before the universe existed?"

Early philosophers proposed some variation of a Prime Mover. Usually, this was a concept of an omnipotent God. Other traditions saw a Fundamental Reality of endless cycles of creation and destruction of all things. Still, others believe the answer is beyond the conceptual understanding of humans and is ultimately unknowable.

I propose the answer is integral to Fundamental Reality, that Fundamental Reality is bound by science, and that all science is knowable. This question is phrased incorrectly. "What existed before anything else," is internally contradictory, plus, the question infers the existence of Time, which did not exist. To address the question properly, I propose the label "X2B," defined as the absence of all things, and the label "2B," defined as the first instance of the cessation of X2B. The question can now be posed as, "What condition, 'Q,' acting on 'X2B' will result in '2B.' "

Concerning Ducks

Once upon a time, two Pekin Ducks came upon a cozy tavern in the woods. They enter and are greeted by a minxy Red Fox Barmaid who asks, "What'll you guys—or gals— have? I can never tell what sex you Pekins are."

The first duck replies, "That's ok. We don' know either. Gimme a Slug 'n Barley."

The second duck replies, "Oh, I believe I would enjoy a Grasshopper in Dandelion Juice, please."

The Barmaid smirks and says, "You got it!" As she purees the dandelion greens, she asks, "Where are you two from?"

The second duck says, "We ask ourselves that very question, but we don't know. We simply enjoy our journey. My name is Yin. This is my companion, Yang."

"Well, welcome, Yin and Yang. You have come to the right place, I betcha." The Barmaid glanced to her left and winked toward the table in the dark corner.

Yin said, "I need to powder my beak. Which way to the relieving area?"

"Out the back door, to the right. Watch your step. There's a big pond of gunk back there."

Yin headed to the back door, leaving Yang nursing his Slug 'n Barley.

The Barmaid asked, "So, you two don't know whether you're guys or gals?

"Naw, we never got the urge to mate and find out. I figure we're both males or both females or sumpin'. We got no idea why we're bonded so tight. Go figure."

"I'll keep the Slugs and Grasshoppers coming."

They heard a splash from the back and then a honk of joy.

The Barmaid said, "Oh-oh. I should have warned Yin about the pond. That's not water. It's where "Boss" keeps his not-used-anymore black writing ink!"

Yang replied, "Yin don't care. It's wet. Yin'll swim in anything. Dive to the bottom and come out wings a-flappin'."

"I'll get some blotting paper—just in case."

Yang turned to face the back door, wing leaning against the bar. Yang picked up his Slug and Barley and waited to see what a solid white Pekin duck that had just gone diving in some old writing ink looked like.

The Barmaid returned with a blotting book to absorb any unwanted ink and laid it on the bar.

Yin, thrilled and excited by an unexpected dip in a pool, walked in wearing nothing but a duck smile and black ink. Yin saw Yang leaning against the bar and stopped cold, staring into his eyes.

Yang stood up, duck-ramrod straight. They stared at one another.

Yang picked up a piece of blotting paper and slowly walked to Yin, who was still standing motionless, staring at Yang.

Yang tenderly wiped the black ink from Yin's beak, leaving only beautiful orange brilliant against a once pure white, now pure black, body.

They stared at one another.

Yang's head suddenly bobbed. Yin parroted.

Yang's head and neck swayed from side to side. Yin parroted.

Yang did a two-step sidestep. Their dance began.

The barmaid watched with approval. She stared toward the darkened corner and said, "Guess we are about to find out, huh, Boss?"

They danced. Oh, how they danced. Bogey and Bacall on Astaire and Roger's feet. Dancing without touching.

Finally, Yang touched the tip of his beak to Yin's. She let him. He placed his beak on top of hers and pushed down for her pleasure. She pushed hers back up against his. Their orange beaks became as one. Innocent love blossoming into something more mature. Their heads finally touched. Sinking into one another—becoming one. His pure white head mixed with her pure black head to create an impressionistic shifting form of the darkest gray.

They danced.

Their necks became entangled, adding to the beautiful abstract texture unfolding on their floor of dance. Their bodies touched. And touched again. Bodies combining. Black and White combining into a beautiful shifting dark grayness of form and texture. Finally, the last vestige of white and the last vestige of black entered the overpowering Dark Gray pulsating orb hanging in the air.

It hung there. Weak merged with Strong. It pulsed.

The Dark Gray turned a bit lighter and pulsed down to a slightly smaller size.

Cold became one with Hot. It pulsed. A bit lighter. A bit smaller.

Dark merged with Light. It pulsed. Lighter. Smaller.

Day merged with Night. Again.

Quiet merged with Loud. And again.

Each Essence merged with its complementary Essence. The orb was now only a point of pulsating soft, almost pure, light. As beautiful as it was virtually imperceptible.

At last, Masculine and Feminine merged. The pulsating light gray orb pulsed into Nothingness.

The barmaid looked into the darkness of the corner as she washed her utensils. She asked, "Did you get what you needed, Boss?"

A disembodied voice spoke inside her fox head, *Maybe.*

A Hypothesis

Since nothing can exist within X2B to change it, and since nothing can exist outside of X2B to act upon it, then we must conclude that X2B still exists and that there can never be 2B. Ipso facto, we do not exist.

And yet ... "I think."

Must we abandon science and resort to magic or mysticism or religion or ...

BOSS! You saw it when you wrote the damned word. It went somewhere! Where did it go? OPEN YOUR EYES! SEE IT!

... is ... *this* the explanation?

X2b is an abstract Mathematical Construct containing only Mathematics and Nothing. When abstract Yin and Yang within X2B spontaneously separate into complementary Essences, "Essence," being abstract, remains within the Mathematical Construct, while the information defining the complementary essences would *not* be abstract, but rather one-dimensional strings. These could not exist within X2B, so Q would be created to contain the one-dimensional strings. Q would expand as all possible Essences discarded their associated one-dimensional string framework into Q. The Essences would remain in X2b.

Each string would seek to reunify with all other strings, but could not reunify since the Essence they defined was no longer in the same construct. This attraction, which we label "Gravity," would pull the strings closer together, thereby increasing compression energy and density. As infinite strings accumulated within Q, Gravity would approach infinity. Since an infinite number is not allowed within the mathematical construct, Q would be required to expel the strings into another Reality. The strings, free from the effects of Gravity in the almost infinitely dense construct, would then vibrate into quantum foam, creating 2B; that is, Space-Time.

"The Boss"
by Foxie

I was lonely.

I called to the voice in my head to see if he would answer. I call it "he," but it may be a "she," "they," or "sexless duck." I don't really know. "Boss" is just my inner dialogue, or maybe a Muse, or maybe a Creator. Who *really* knows?

"Send in the ducks, Boss. I'm lonely. It's been quiet around here."

I've been busy. I'm sorry. You have an active mind. It needs challenges. Maybe I can have you write a novel.

"I love books! But I'm a fox and don't have an opposable thumb. I can't write."

I'll send you infinite monkeys with typewriters.

"Oh, no! Not infinite anything. I learned my lesson. A single monkey that can take dictation will be more than satisfactory." The voice inside my head laughed. I had never heard him laugh before.

Very well. A trained monkey and a typewriter. How about a male fox?

"Oh, Boss. Can you do that? Can he be tall and handsome?"

Let's go one better. You make him the protagonist in your novel and have him manifest out of his story into your story. Rushdie did it with less to work with. You can, too. You won't need me anymore. How 'bout that?

Now, *I* laughed. "That sounds a little bit like 'magic.' I thought you didn't allow magic in your stories."

These would be your stories. Write them as you must. Besides, when you imagine a thing, you create the thing. A parallel universe. A multidimensional world. Virtual reality. Maybe Collapsing Wave Functions that collapse into

~ 39 ~

something wild—like two ducks manifesting into Nothingness in one reality and out of Nothingness in another.

I'll write "The Never-Ending Monkey" story for you.

"The Never-Ending Monkey"

Once upon a time, a Monkey carrying a typewriter came upon a cozy tavern in the woods. He entered and sat down at the end of the long bar. He set a typewriter in front of him and began typing.

A minxy Red Fox barmaid walked over and said what'll you have, Monkey?"

"A Banana Daiquiri. Heavy on the banana."

"You got it!" She began preparing the daiquiri—heavy on the banana.

He continued typing away but suddenly stopped, and exclaimed, "I got nothin'. Nothin'!"

The barmaid delivered the daiquiri and asked, "Writer's block?"

"Yea. Permanent writer's block. I got nothin' left to say."

She laughed. "Write my Autobiography. Authorized Edition!"

Yeah. I could do that. How does it begin?"

"How 'bout, 'Once upon a time, a large, handsome fox with a magnificent tail came upon a cozy tavern in the woods.' "

The Monkey began typing furiously. "Good. Good. Got it! Then what happens?"

The barmaid laughed. "Use my imagination!"

Author's Statement
by Foxie

I told Boss that the concept of "Nothing" separating into complementary Essences to create Q is more scientific than the concept of Luminiferous Aether, and even the Theory of Relativity couldn't completely kill off *that* concept.

Boss reluctantly agreed.

He sounded sad but resigned. *It's a start, I suppose. 'Luminiferous Aether farted.' It's the best I can do.*

I replied out loud, "It's your 'Q!' Boss. A Quack in Space! And don't be vulgar."

He laughed. That was the last time I ever heard his voice.

As for my Autobiography, it goes on. My soulmate, Teumessian, had completed his tour in Greek Mythology and was out searching for the meaning of the Universe and everything in it. He found *me*.

Sometimes, I sit at my corner table in the darkness, looking out over my little tavern, philosophizing. Teumessian encourages me. Men are so simple, tunnel-visioned, I suppose.

I once said to him, "I don't think Boss ever understood the equivalence of his X2B and Mathematics. Mathematics would exist even if nothing else existed. X2b never ceased—it expanded to include 2B. All things emerge from Mathematics ... don't you think?"

His ears stood up, and his tail twitched as he stared into nothingness and considered my suggestion.

He excites me so.

This doesn't answer everything, of course ... but it's the best I can do.

FADE OUT

Disembodied voice with a British Accent: "You were correct, Hammy. That IS the question!"

 # CUT #

###

FIVE

THE ANSWER
A Scientific Fantasy on Themes by Zarathustra, Spinoza, and Planck

by Dennis Wammack (c) 2013

One

Reality, as we perceive it, is incomplete and is not a fundamental property of the universe. It evolved from, and is limited to, our subjective experiences necessary for survival. This Perceived Reality is emergent from Experience interacting with the phenomena of Biology.

Biology is emergent from Chemistry, which is emergent from Physics, which is emergent from one-dimensional vibrating Strings in their holding construct, Mathematics.

The first three phenomena exist in Newtonian Space-Time. Strings and Mathematics exist at the quantum level.

Time is an emergent property from the interaction between Mathematics and Physics.

Experience is imprinted on a String as the String emerges through higher phenomena. Strings had no Experience at Time-Zero of The Big Bang.

Consciousness is the aggregate Experience of a collection of Strings.

Gravity is the physical attraction of a String to all other Strings; all seeking reunification as they existed before The Big Bang.

Collective-Consciousness is the aggregate Experience of all Strings composing a Universe. It is Fundamental Reality.

Mathematics is the zero-dimensional holding construct for all Evaporation Events as defined in Part Three.

From the short story
Empty Glass

Late into the night, the writer sat on his backyard bench beside Buddha, drinking fine cognac and chatting with a hallucination.

The hallucination, whose name was Bubba, asked, "So, other than the Amalek thing, which verse do you find most challenging?"

The writer thoughtfully sipped Bubba's cognac and answered, "I guess Genesis three-something where God said, 'Man has eaten from the Tree of Knowledge and now knows good and evil, but I won't allow him to eat from the Tree of Life and live forever.'

"The 'Tree of Knowledge' metaphor is obvious, but ... 'The Tree of Life?' What the hell is that about?"

Two

We were born sixteen billion years ago.

Our mother produced many eggs throughout her existence. We label her eggs, "Black Holes." The mass of a black hole is so dense that nothing, not even light, can escape its gravitational pull.

When the gravity of a black hole captures a passing body, it pulls the body across the black hole's "Event Horizon," where the information carried by the body is stripped away and incorporated into the event horizon. What remains of the body are vibrating strings. These strings are pulled to the center of the black hole, where the space between the vibrating strings is reduced, thereby decreasing their vibration amplitude and increasing their compression energy.

The density of the black hole increases.

From the short story
Country Light

Her youth was as wonderful as a country girl's could be.

In the spring, wild violets covered the fields. Summer came when her feet were so toughened that she could walk the gravel roads without feeling the gravel. In the fall, the sun shining through the trees turned each leaf into a celebration of life and color. She would stand staring, mesmerized by the riot of color, amazed at the interplay of leaves and light. Clouds and trees always brought her joy.

It made her feel closer to God.

Three

As the density of a black hole approaches infinity, its entropy approaches zero. At zero entropy, no strings would vibrate, compression energy would be infinite, and the concept of space-time would be meaningless.

Neither infinite mass nor zero entropy is mathematically, and therefore physically, possible. To circumvent this condition, as infinite mass is reached, the black hole *Evaporates* and ceases to exist in the *Mother Universe*. Concurrent with, and resulting from this *Evaporation Event*, a new space-time continuum, that is, *Universe*, is born external to the *Mother Universe*.

From the short story
The Naming

The homeless dog, Jake, lay with his head in a large stand of monkey grass. His eyes looked upward. They were fastened on the large tree, full of leaves, on which the sun poured forth its light. He was fascinated by the interplay of light and leaves. The tree, a living thing, full of movement and energy.

His female companion, Riley, sat on her haunches monitoring the street. One never knew when food might pass by. A child with ice cream, a workman with a bag of delights, someone with a sack of groceries. She glanced toward Jake. Her eyes followed his gaze into the tree as she thought, 'No food there, not even a squirrel to chase. To where does his mind wander? What would he do without me?'

Jake sighed and looked once more into the glory of the light. It seemed to him that the leaves were sending stardust back to the Sun.

He closed his eyes to dream dog dreams.

Four

At an *Evaporation Event*, the mass of the evaporated black hole condenses into the nearest suitable zero-dimensional *Mathematics* construct. Its Event Horizon is not transmitted.

At Time-Zero in the birth of a *Universe*, Space-Time measurements are at Planck-Level initialization points, and the compression force stored in each string is released, resulting in an expansion process whereby the collection of strings sublimate into an assortment of subatomic particles, creating quantum foam.

Each *String*, however, remains bound to every other *String* by *Gravity*.

The new universe evolves based on the values of its twenty-seven Universal Constants. Most births are short-lived because variation from optimum in any one of these values will restrict expansion, and the universe can no longer evolve. Our Universal Constants are identical to our mothers. We continue to exist.

The common label for the birth of our universe is The Big Bang. A more appropriate label would be *The Birth of the Tree of Life*.

from the short story
Dorothy and The Quantum Mechanic

Dorothy stood in her backyard and gazed at her magnificent Oak tree. The balmy wind of a dark afternoon rustled the new spring leaves on the great tree. The dark clouds parted, suddenly bathing the tree in brilliant light. She was momentarily overcome with the glory of the leaves embracing the sun.

She tried to find the soul of a leaf but did not know where to look. "Silly woman," she thought. Still, she tried to become one with the tree.

She almost could.

Five

From our explosive birth, all that was and is, began to grow and expand. The Tree of Life grew as it created quanta of energy, of light, of matter. Eventually, this great trunk grew into interstellar dust, and galaxies formed. Within galaxies, solar systems formed. And planets and moons. On planets that contained water, life formed. If conditions allowed, life became ever increasingly complex, leading to intelligence. Regardless of intelligence, however, all matter is interconnected, simply different twigs of the same limb.

Our local limb is our sun and all that our sun influences and produces. The Earth is but one of our sun's children. Earth has produced abundant and varied life, different types, and many species. All life on Earth is interconnected. Each member of a species is simply a different leaf on the same twig.

from the short story
The Peace of Bark

Footsie trotted beside his adopted master toward the great brick building named 'Church.'

Upon arriving, the two strode to the giant tree where Footsie obediently lay down to wait for his master to fulfill his rituals inside the Church. His master removed the leash and laid it by the tree so that no one would mistake Footsie for the stray dog he had been before finding his "forever home." The man scratched Footsie's ear, said "Good dog," and hurried to join the others as they entered the church.

Footsie luxuriated in the comforting smells, sights, and noise of humans. He wrapped himself in the glorious surroundings of sky, wind, scent, and earth. It was as if everything and every creature were connected.

Laying his head upon his front paws and closing his eyes, he felt that every homeless creature who had ever lived had just found their forever home.

Six

Time has no physical existence. It is an entity's interpretation of a higher phenomenon. This higher phenomenon is the collapse and reformation of *Probability Wave Functions*.

Probability Waves form, propagate, and collapse. When a *Probability Wave Function* collapses and reforms, the interface between the collapse and the reformation is an entity's interpretation of the passage of *Time*.

The collapse of the wave is influenced by and experienced by all entities who cause or observe the collapse. This *Experience* is imprinted on all *Strings* associated with the collapsed wave function. A label for the cumulative *Experiences* of an individual *String* is *Soul.*

Reality at the Newtonian level is not fundamental to the universe but is only a localized construct of an entity. *Fundamental Reality* is the aggregate *Experience* of all *Strings*; that is, the *Souls* of all *Strings*; that is, *Collective-Consciousness.*

Time masks an entity's perception of *Fundamental Reality.* Upon death, the entity no longer passes through *Time.* It exists only at the quantum level. Its perception of *Fundamental Reality* is no longer masked. Death is not the termination of *Consciousness* but rather the unmasking of the entity's aggregate *Soul* to *Fundamental Reality.*

All Strings are ultimately interconnected at Time-Zero of The Big Bang. As The Tree of Life is the Body of God, so then is Fundamental Reality Collective-Consciousness the Mind of God.

from the short story
Genesis: We Begin

Adam lay without feeling on his son's grave. Void of all emotion, Adam stared into the brilliant, moonless firmament. He remembered that he had never answered Breathson's question: "Father, can something come back to life after it is killed?"

He had replied, "That is a good question. I shall ask those far wiser than myself."

"Well, Son, are you now far wiser than me? Do you now know the answer? Does the rabbit live?"

Tears seeped from Adam's eyes. Exhausted and with a blank mind, he fell toward unconscious sleep.

Unto Adam, Breathson said, "The rabbit lives. I live. We are the light. We are free from the burden of the flesh that carried our souls. Our souls experience all we have ever experienced, and we know all we have ever known. I now know the soul of the rabbit, experienced its joy of life, its fears, its death. And, to the limit of its experience, it knows mine. Once we were bound and blinded by the flesh. Now we are no longer bound. Now we are no longer blind. Now, not only are we alive, at last, we live."

Seven

"Do unto others as you would have them do unto you."

Philosophers teach us *how* to be good.

Herein is the *why*: A person is not far removed from their parents, children, spouse, teachers, and friends. Our attraction or repulsion is great even at the Newtonian level. At the quantum level, these bonds are much stronger. *Souls* are connected by their mutual *Experiences* so that not only are we aware of the experience of our own *Soul*, but we also experience the *Souls* of those to whom we are connected. We experience that which they experienced. 'What you do unto others' is literally what you do unto yourself. Forever.

Such is *The Tree of Life*, where all life and all things are connected. And everything experiences that which is experienced by everything to which it is connected. You have only to die to live forever.

The Tree of Life can be glimpsed through concepts of quantum mechanics, the nature of time, and the expanding universe. Until this was understood, the nature of *The Tree of Life* was hidden from the understanding of our kind.

Now, we can understand that *The Tree of Life* is the "Living Universe" composed of everything in it.

from the short story
Joshua Maximus: The Gospel According to the Storyteller

Upon the cross, Joshua answered each daemon of weakness, "I am who I am. I am not bound by earthly flesh. You cannot control me. I shall pass into the highest heaven. I shall enter the majestic glory of the one God. I will preach to the dead. I will teach the prophets. All who wish can come to me. I will show them the Light which is the Way." They came to him. In his mind, in his heart, in his soul— the prophets, the poor, the sick, the lame, the sinners, the lost, the oppressed. He taught them. He showed them the Light.

Eight

As The Big Bang was the birth of the Tree of Life, so, too, was it the birth of God. At birth, God was unformed and without experience or knowledge. To obtain those things, God would have to live and grow and learn and evolve. How long? A billion years? A trillion years? In a place without time, what difference? All strings composing The Tree of Life reconnect at their point of birth, connecting with knowledge of all that would ever happen. Could ever happen. God is self-aware of every quantum of its being, every experience, every possibility.

The moment of its birth connects seamlessly with the moment of its death. Fully formed, all parts are self-aware, accessing all experience, all emotion, all pain, all suffering, all joy, all love, all death. All life. These things will be known because a part knows, and every part is known to every other part. All will be eternal because in this place, there is no time. All time that has ever been will have passed, encapsulated in its awareness.

All things join as one. Celebrating every part of its being. It is eternal. It is The All. It is The One. It is beyond comprehension.

Nine

"What's it all about?"

The answer is this: "You."

You will die. Your soul will be fully formed. You will access your Soul, all of your "Nows," simultaneously. You will access the souls of all people and things with which you are connected. Your knowledge, your experience, and your emotions will be accessible and experienced by all who precede you.

What did you expect? That you would leave nothing but dust? Be reborn as a person half your dying age to live in a mansion in the sky on a street of gold? Reborn a bug? Seventy-two houris?

Know this: Your experience is not a perishable commodity evaporating on your death. Your consciousness does not cease at death but rather can then recognize the continuum of your existence. Regardless of your good works or your bad deeds, regardless of faith, regardless of having done evil or good, all your pain, your fear, your weaknesses, your shortcomings, your prejudices, your evils, your triumphs, your strengths, your joys, your loves — these things live and are known to God.

But how would God know these things if not through you? If not because of you? If it had not been experienced by you?

You will die and shed your body and become the timeless presence of all things that have ever been.

You will join The All—The One. You will become God.

Be worthy.

###

###

SCRATCHING SCHRODINGER'S CAT

by Dennis Wammack © 2024, 2025

His wife of fifty-plus years walked him to the table on their deck overlooking the backyard.

He sat down, glanced over his kingdom, smiled at his wife, and said, "Poked, pinched, prodded, and I've got to wait two weeks for the results."

She replied, "I'll bring you coffee. Trust God. Everything will be fine." She left him to make coffee.

Brighteyes surreptitiously peered around the corner of the house in search of chipmunks. The cat belonged to the neurosurgeon who lived down the street, Ansel Schrodinger. His wife had named the cat Brighteyes before she found out its real name was Erwin.

The man referred to Erwin as "Schrodinger's Cat." His wife never understood the hilarity of the name, no matter how many times he mansplained his version of quantum mechanics.

Brighteyes, detecting no chipmunks, ambled onto the deck, tail twitching high in the air. He looked at the man and decided to grace him with his presence.

The man leaned down and held out his hand.

Brighteyes entered its "Yes, you may scratch me" mode and walked toward him.

The man smiled as he looked into the cat's eyes and extended his fingers to scratch its head. Your eyes aren't very bright today, Brighteyes. "Deadeyes" might be more appropriate.

His fingers touched the cat's arched head. *Jesus!*

The man looked into Forever. *Planets. Solar systems. Constellations. Galaxies. Universes.*

Mesmerized, he looked deeper. *Blackness. Lights. Points. Expanding. Exploding. Contracting. Existing. Not Existing.*

Deeper. *Kaleidoscopes. Colors. Shapes. All things. No things. Pulsating.*

He closed his eyes and threw up.

His wife walked onto the deck, dropped the coffee, and ran to him. "Honey, what's wrong? Can you stand up? Can you get into the house?"

She took her husband's arm and helped him to the living room sofa to lie down. She said, "I'll get a wet towel. Lie still."

The scene played out as such scenes play out.

Two days passed.

His wife helped him to the table on their deck overlooking their backyard.

She said, "I'll bring you coffee. If you have the least sensation of vertigo, call me. You have meds. Understand?"

He understood.

As she left to prepare his coffee, he leaned back, breathed in the cool spring air, and waited in wary anticipation. *All right, Brighteyes, where are you?*

Dr. Schrodinger's cat ambled onto the deck.

The man leaned down and put out his hand to Brighteyes. He extended his fingers to scratch the cat's head as he looked into the cat's dead, lifeless eyes. *Your eyes still aren't right, cat. "Deadeyes" would be better."*

His fingers touched the cat's arched head. This time, he was prepared. He stared into the cat. *Forever. Blackness. Light. Points. Expanding. Exploding. Contracting. Existing. Not Existing.*

Through his nausea, the man began to recognize the shifting, kaleidoscopic colors, shapes, and patterns were Brighteyes. Brighteyes as a kitten. Brighteyes as a strong young cat. Brighteyes, the stealthy hunter. Brighteyes, a monster waiting to pounce on a chipmunk. Brighteyes' life. All at once. In fast-forward. In frozen snapshots. Rewinding. Brighteyes as he really is.

The man considered looking deeper into the cat's eyes but decided he was not yet ready. He withdrew his hand and called out, "Honey! Bring those meds!"

Twelve days passed.

The husband and wife, back from the Doctor's visit, sat on their deck drinking afternoon coffee, talking.

He said, "I'm sorry we can't travel. I've screwed you out of our trip to Paris."

She replied, "We've been before. Sitting here with you is all I want right now."

"They said meds will control the pain, but still … our quality of life is in the crapper, and the kid's inheritance will be shot. I'm so sorry. I'll do the best I can, but the sooner I croak, the better.

"Don't joke about it! Please!"

He laughed. "You're right. Go fix dinner. I'm tired, but I'm fine."

He squeezed her hand as she rose to leave. "Love you, Hon."

"I love you, too." She leaned over and kissed his forehead.

He waited.

It came.

His fingers touched the cat's arched head. *Forever. Blackness. Light. Points. Expanding. Exploding. Contracting. Existing. Not Existing.*

He saw the cat complete. Not an incomplete perceived reality but rather the cat's fundamental reality. He looked deeper into the kaleidoscopic colors and shapes of the collection of vibrating strings he had labeled "Schrodinger's Cat." *Colors dissolving. Formless forms. Bubbling foam of color-saturated vibrating strings. Strings vibrating into everything.*

He gazed deeper, beneath the carpet of vibrating foam.

The white light was beautiful beyond knowing. It spoke to him. *"I am the Light. The All and the One."*

Another voice within the light said, *"You are not yet required to remain. You may return, if you wish."*

His younger voice said, *"Nah. Stay here, man. We had a great run. No need spendin' our savings on a couple of pain-filled months. Shed our body. Come on down."*

His older voice agreed, *"That's true. Low return on investment. Release our body. It's time to live."*

The man decided. He scratched Erwin's head as he stared still deeper into the beautiful pulsating white light. *This isn't the way I expected to go.*

His wife of fifty-plus years found him lying face down on the deck.

Schrodinger's cat sat on his head, contentedly licking its paw.

###

SEVEN

DOROTHY
AND THE QUANTUM MECHANIC

by Dennis Wammack (c) 2014

1. Dorothy
The Days of Her Life

Dorothy sat in her rocking chair watching the classic movie channel. Oxygen pumped into her nostrils. It was two o'clock. She wasn't concerned if it was a.m. or p.m. The TV shows were good. She would watch and doze. She would sometimes reach down to stroke Fritzi's head, and then remember Fritzi had died long ago. She missed her dog. She had been a wonderful companion.

People told Dorothy that she should get out more. They told her that she should do this, that she should do that.

One did not tell Dorothy what to do. Dorothy knew what to do. She had spent her life working for governors and judges and authors and lawyers. It was unfortunate that she had never had tea with the Queen. The Queen would have had such a lovely time.

Dorothy knew what to do. Snorting oxygen and watching classic movies was what to do. If only Fritzi were there.

1. The Quantum Mechanic
The Nature of Time

There is no known reason why time flows in only one direction. As a matter of fact, physicists tell us that time can flow backward as easily as it can flow forward. There appears to be a catch, however. Time flows backward only at the quantum level. At the Newtonian level, time flows only forward. No one knows why.

I believe the physicists to be in error. I believe time can never flow backward at any level.

Did you know that color does not exist in nature? Color is a brain's interpretation of a higher physical phenomenon, electromagnetic radiation in this case. When electromagnetic radiation of a wavelength we can observe—that is, "light"—falls on an object, part of the radiation is absorbed, and part is reflected. If the object reflects only red wavelengths of radiation, receptors in our eyes respond to the reflected 650-nanometer wavelength of the electromagnetic radiation and send a signal to our brains. The brain labels this signal "red," and we say the object is "red."

The same is true of sound. Sound does not exist in nature; vibrating molecules exist in nature. A device is needed to capture the frequency and intensity of the vibrating molecules. These vibrating molecules, when transmitted to an eardrum, cause the eardrum to vibrate. The eardrum sends a signal to the brain. The brain interprets these vibrations as "sound."

I mention the nature of color and sound as a prelude to this statement: time may not exist in nature. "Time" may be the brain's interpretation of a higher physical phenomenon. Scientists do not know the nature of this phenomenon.

I do. It is this: "Time is the interface between the total collapse of probability wave functions in a set of quanta and the re-forming of these probability wave functions to a totally uncollapsed set." The brain interprets this interface as "time."

2. Dorothy
In The Beginning

Dorothy woke from her brief snooze. She was delighted. It was two in the morning, and a movie was about to start, a classic —"Lassie Come Home," one of her favorites. The ever-present hum of the oxygen generator serenaded the room.

She reached down to stroke Fritzi's head. Fritzi wasn't there.

The light came.

It was incomprehensibly beautiful. So brilliant you would be blinded if you needed eyes with which to see it. The presence was overpowering — with warmth, with comfort, with joy, with strength. Within the light, she saw her big brother, her beloved mother, and her dear father. She saw her husband, so handsome in his uniform. She saw family and friends she had not seen in years. And there was Fritzi—and Lady, and Little Bit, and Schneptse. How could this be?

This was not imagination, not delusion. This was real! This was more real than life itself. She held her breath.

The light seemed to reach out to her. Dorothy sighed a great sigh.

2. The Quantum Mechanic
The Practical Effect of the Nature of Time

Not only can time not flow backward, but there is neither time nor the concept of time in the past. The very notion is meaningless. The physical phenomenon that gives the perception of time does not exist in the past. There are no uncollapsed probability wave functions in the past. They have all collapsed. This is what got us into the present.

A poor analogy for time is that it is like a large soap bubble. Time exists only on the surface of the bubble. There is no time inside the bubble: all probability wave functions have collapsed. There is no time outside the bubble: no probability wave functions have collapsed.

But the bubble analogy is limiting, because time is a local event, more tectonic than wave-like. This is what allows us to see inside probability waves. There is no time within the probability wave. Experiments observing collapsing wave functions are peering into a space without time. Time exists only at the wave's collapse. Immediately upon perception, the instant collapses into all previous instances, where all instances exist simultaneously.

Ray Cummings, science fiction writer, was correct when he wrote: "Time is what keeps everything from happening at once."

But having happened, it is all happening at once.

3. Dorothy
Born Again

Darkness. Solitude. Calm. Comfort. Peace. Protection. Love. Togetherness. Connections.

Blinding light then formed images which quickly dissolved into incomprehensible, unfocused, shifting impressions. The images flowed sideways and then with no direction; no up, no down. They whirled, folded back into themselves; chaotic, formless, unknowable, uncontrollable.

Darkness. Unconsciousness. Unknowing. Resetting. Programming. Analyzing. Recognizing. Remembering.

She focused on something part remembrance and part pulsating chaos. It was light coming through a window. She focused. She retrieved.

She held a sliver of the remembrance. It was surrounded by kaleidoscopic images within kaleidoscopic images, but the remembrance was knowable. It was light coming through the window, falling on her mother's face.

She willed the remembered sliver of her mother, warm and comforting. The kaleidoscopic chaos of remembrance whirled through her, around her, everywhere. But she held onto the memory of her mother in the kitchen making a cake. She captured and organized the bits and pieces of the chaos until she once again experienced the moment.

The chaos stopped. All was still. She experienced her mother in the kitchen baking a cake. Light spilled through the kitchen window. A mockingbird sang. Every detail was magnified. Heightened. The beauty of the moment was overwhelming. Why had she not recognized it then? This was not memory. This was actually then. She shifted her focus. Another coherent memory came to her.

She shifted her focus—another memory. She shifted it again and again. She relived every experience. Holding it. Glorying in it. The joy. Why had she never recognized it? Embraced it? Why had she ever been afraid? Unsure? She relived her life's experiences moment-by-moment and in entirety. She saw herself and finally knew herself. She was Dorothy, Dorothy of the unending days.

3. The Quantum Mechanic
The Nature of the Soul

Is there such a thing as a soul? Can science even suggest that such a thing exists, much less quantify it?

Perhaps. Perhaps not.

Nonetheless, it is this: "A soul is the record of the collection of entangled quanta as its probability wave functions collapse and reform."

One end of a soul is capped by the moment of its viability, the other by its moment of termination. It is a collection of long tubes, entangled together, inside of which is maintained the history of what each wave function collapsed into. This information is decodable by any entity that experiences the cross-section of the tubes for any given time frame. These tubes, however, do not have the dimension commonly identified as "length" because "time" is no longer a concept associated with events having already occurred.

People touch, have common experiences, exchange information, affect one another. People are connected, some with great passion, some by great hatred, some by casual acquaintance. Their souls are connected because they shared a moment. All things have souls. Rocks tend to simply sit somewhere, tending their space, just existing. The soul of a human is far more interesting than the soul of a rock. But then again, maybe that's not true in stories told by rocks.

A soul is incomplete—it is not accessible—it does not become whole—until its host is no longer experiencing time.

4. Dorothy
Considerations

Dorothy considered every moment of her life. She forgave herself for her weaknesses and her wrongdoings. She forgave everyone she had ever known. There was no such thing as guilt, only human experience. She gloried in the triumphs and the beauty of each person. She could consider any moment in her life that she chose to consider. She considered Fritzi as a puppy, Fritzi lying asleep on the sofa.

She considered when she had adopted Lady, an old dog who had come wandering into her life. Lady had been in search of a master. Dorothy became her master—her savior. Dorothy had always wondered what Lady's story was. The dog, like Dorothy, had been very dignified. She had certainly had many litters of puppies. She certainly had a story.

Dorothy considered Lady when they had first met. Dorothy and Lady had looked at one another. A bond had formed. They were connected. Dorothy considered the moment. She focused, then focused harder. The blackness came. This time, Dorothy had the experience and the skills to capture the whirling fragments. She pieced the fragments into a moment that she could consider. She considered each moment in Lady's illustrious life. She considered Lady's soul.

So obvious, so right, so easily done. Dorothy considered the souls of everyone she had ever known, of everyone to whom she had ever been connected. Not as a voyeur, not as a spy, but as a part of their existence—to heal their wounds, to wrap them in compassion and understanding. Time was of no consequence to Dorothy. In this place, there is no time.

She saw life from her husband's perspective, from her brother's, from her mother's, and from her father's. She experienced their experiences, thought their thoughts, acquired their knowledge, and suffered their pains.

She incorporated their experience into hers.

4. The Quantum Mechanic
Leaves

Information and processes at the quantum level and the Newtonian level can be exchanged. The basic requirement for life is created at the quantum level, the generation of oxygen by plants. Sunlight falls on a leaf, and the leaf's chlorophyll converts the sunlight into oxygen. This occurs at the quantum level. It is mind-boggling—sunlight converted into oxygen.

We, of course, can convert hydrogen into sub-atomic particles and big explosions. We can even make atoms spell IBM.

We are extremely clever. A leaf, I think, is more so.

5. Dorothy
The Tree

A favorite moment for Dorothy to consider was one of solitude and quietness. She stood in the yard of the home she shared with her husband. For no particular reason, she was gazing at the magnificent oak in their backyard. The balmy wind of a dark afternoon rustled the new spring leaves on the great tree. The dark clouds parted; the sun suddenly bathed the tree in brilliant sunlight. She felt the ecstasy of the leaves. She felt the warmth and rejoicing and the wonder and the glory that the leaves felt. She tried to find the soul of a leaf but did not know where to look—how to empathize with it, how to embrace it. She considered caterpillars and wondered if they could find a leaf's soul. "Silly woman," she thought. But she almost envied the leaves and their affair with the sun.

She tried to consider the soul of the tree. She could almost find it. She almost felt like a leaf on some majestic tree.

5. The Quantum Mechanic
The Nature of the Universe

Every student of solid geometry knows that through any single point, three lines can pass that are perpendicular to one another, no more, no less.

Students of "N-Dimensional Analysis" know that through any single point, an infinite number of lines can pass that are perpendicular to one another. Thought to be strictly a mathematical construct, what if this does apply to the physical universe?

When writers speak of parallel universes, I believe them to be in error. I believe universes aren't parallel. I believe they are perpendicular.

A probability wave function collapses into everything it is possible for it to collapse into. It simply propagates into perpendicular universes. It just does not, as a rule, propagate very far. When these realities become internally inconsistent, then the probability wave function cannot re-form. "Time" cannot occur, and that particular perpendicular universe simply stops propagating. That may be where all our missing dark matter and energy are located—in universes branching off, perpendicular to ours.

All possibilities are tried. Virtually all fail to propagate. Our physical laws and universal constants are what they are because our dimension has remained internally consistent from the beginning.

Very few dimensions can remain internally consistent for very long. Very few dimensions will continue to propagate for a long period. And ours? Ours is on a roll.

6. Dorothy
End of Days

Dorothy considered her end of days. She always stood there, of course. Just as she always stood at every other moment of her life, and at every moment of every soul she had ever considered. Within Dorothy was the knowledge and experience of the lives and souls of everyone she had ever touched, of everyone she had ever known.

Dorothy looked upon the woman in the chair watching television and reaching for a dog that wasn't there. She looked upon her with overwhelming love and compassion, with the warmth and the glow of a life well lived, of a soul well formed. She had been blind, but now she could see. She had been deaf, but now she could hear.

To the woman sitting in the chair watching television, Dorothy held out her arms.

6. The Quantum Mechanic
In The Beginning

A black hole is so dense that not even light can escape its gravitational force. As more mass is captured, the entropy of the black hole increases, and its compression increases.

Eventually, the black hole captures passing mass and compresses out all information in the additional mass. Nothing remains except motionless one-dimensional strings packed with no space between them. There is no time, no motion, no vibration—there is no space within which to move. The black hole is now of maximum possible mass, minimum possible size, and maximum entropy.

The Mother Universe is now ready to give birth.

A passing mass captured. The additional mass compresses the strings within the black hole out of existence and into another place. The strings, pushed to another place, are now released from the unimaginable compression of the black hole. The unimaginable compressive force is no longer binding them together. Free of the compression, the strings vibrate—probability wave functions form, collapse, reform. Time begins.

All strings follow the original string into the other place. All strings burst forth, vibrating, forming probability wave functions. All quanta, all energy, all mass, all things are connected back to this single occurrence.

Aristotle and Saint Thomas Aquinas were quite correct; there was an original mover.

7. Dorothy
In The Beginning

The light came.

It was incomprehensibly beautiful. So brilliant you would be blinded if you needed eyes with which to see it. The presence was overpowering with warmth, with comfort, with joy, with strength. Within the light, she saw her big brother, her beloved mother, and her dear father. She saw her husband, so handsome in his uniform. She saw family and friends she had not seen in years. And there was Fritzi, and Lady, and Little Bit, and Schneptse. How could this be?

This was not imagination, not delusion. This was real! This was more real than life itself. She held her breath. The light seemed to reach out to her. Dorothy sighed a great sigh.

Her soul burst forth.

###

###

EIGHT

COUNTRY LIGHT

by Dennis Wammack (c) 2013

1. Doggerel for a Christmas Tree

I
gave
a party.
Everyone came.
I sang to their babies,
adults played their games.
Smiles and joy spread all around.
Laughter, shouting, talking abound.
Some left too early, they just couldn't stay.
But always more after. I knew each one by name.
Enough food to feed them. A good time for all.
I gave a party.
And still it
goes on.

2. We Had A Party, Didn't We?

She sank deep into the chair. She would sit for just a minute by the fireplace. There really wasn't much left to do. The girls had cleaned the kitchen, the boys had taken out the trash.

She wasn't used to being this tired. Yes, it had been a long day, but she hadn't really done very much. Baking the ham didn't take long; making the breakfast eggs and biscuits was routine. A couple of pies and a cake, and she was pretty much through, except for corn and peas and the casseroles. The girls had bought most of the food. Mike fried the turkey; the boys sliced the ham and put up the lights. Oh, she had made mac and cheese for the children. And pizza.

Widowed for all of these years, she tried to keep the parties as festive as they had been when her husband had added so much zest and life to them. And, oh, what a party it had been this day. As good as the old days. Her recent Old Days, of course. Not her old Old Days. Grace thought of her Mother. She had died so young. Grace thought about how it must have been.

3. Her old Old Days

Her Mother lay dying. "Mama, promise me you will adopt Grace. Promise me."

"Child, Roscoe will take care of your child just like it was his'n."

"No, Ma, it's hard times. It's hard times, and he will favor his own child over mine. Promise me."

"Papa and me will take care of Grace, I promise you, child."

"No, Mama. Adopt her. Make her your daughter for real."

"Child... child..."

"Mama, please."

4. Shooting Stars

The gas fire burned low. You didn't need face protectors like back then. Back then, the fires were hot. They were real fires.

A shooting star passed through her mind, from back to front, landing as an ember in the front of her mind. Only it wasn't a shooting star. It was Mama.

That was funny. Mama, so long gone... A shooting star.

She should get up now and go on to bed. She had to open up tomorrow. They had decided not to close the extra day. Everyone said times were hard these days.

How comfortable she had grown. Not even her grandchildren believed that she had really walked barefoot to school, or that it was her job to milk the cows before breakfast, before she could go to school even. How extremely lucky she had been to get an education.

She was so fortunate. She remembered Mama and Papa ... how hard they worked. Her grandparents had officially adopted her, making her officially their daughter. They'd loved her very much, even if they weren't her biological parents. Theirs was not the touchy-feely, laughing kind of love, but rather, the 'give the extra potato to their daughter rather than eating it yourself' kind of love. They had already raised ten of their own children during hard times. Grace was the eleventh. The nature of love changes with time.

Her aunts, who had now become her sisters, had married and were raising their own families. She'd had plenty of cousins to play with, and her younger half-sister lived just down the road. There was family enough, even if her real momma and daddy were not around.

Some years, the state would buy gravel off their land for surfacing the county roads. That was always welcome money. There would be extra penny candy at Christmas. She had always gotten wonderful presents. So many Christmases, so many.

5. Spirit of Christmas Past

She remembered her favorite childhood Christmas. Cold, bitter wind had been blowing up through the cracks between the planks in the floor. She huddled toward the fire. What a wonderful day it had been. Everyone had come, Docia and Effie and Minnie and everyone. There had been plenty to eat. A hog had been slaughtered and chickens had been cleaned, and there were biscuits with plenty of butter for everyone. She had gotten wonderful presents ... apples and cashew nuts and so much penny candy that she could eat a whole piece at a time instead of saving and savoring small, single bites. And the very best gift ever ... Papa had carved her a wooden doll out of a piece of leftover four-by-four. It was a wonderful doll, and beautiful. She held the doll close to her, under the blanket to keep it warm, to nurture, to love. The hard, unyielding wood made not a sound of displeasure. Not a grunt of tired, bothered overwork. She loved the doll. It was hers. She held it close to keep it warm. "Does itt'l baby luv his mommy? Mommy luvs her ittl' baby."

Her youth was as wonderful as a country girl's could be. In the spring, wild violets covered the fields. Summer came when your feet were so toughened that you could walk the gravel roads without feeling the gravel. In the fall, the sun would shine through the trees, turning each leaf into a celebration of life and color. She would stand staring, mesmerized by the riot of color. She had been so blessed as a child. So blessed.

6. Learning to Love

The decisive moment of her life came and went unnoticed. Her decision defined who she was and who she would be. In the tenth grade, she was still somewhat shy, not having as many writing tablets and pencils as some of her classmates. She had spoken nicely to one of the more popular girls. The girl had responded with an uppity, curt reply. Grace was left standing alone, wondering why the girl had replied to her that way.

Grace's response was far more mature than she would ever realize. "I'm not going to let her attitude change the way I am, or the way I think, or the way things are supposed to be." She decided to like the girl, whether she wanted to be liked or not. Her eyes were open, and she could see. "Everyone deserves to be loved."

Grace had become Grace.

7. Her Education

Papa, it was Papa. Shooting brightly across her mind, landing with the others, three inches behind her eyes. Papa.

In his last years, Papa had a stroke. It was Grace's responsibility to quit school and help Mama take care of Papa. She was disappointed, of course, but it wasn't horrible to not finish school in those days; but it would have been wonderful to be a high school graduate.

Her teacher seemed distraught when she learned that Grace would not be returning to school the next year. That summer, a car pulled up to Mama and Papa's house. It was her teacher with the school principal. The principal told Mama, "Grace must return to school next year. She has the potential to become a person of great standing. Find a way for her to return to school and graduate."

Mama was impressed that an important man like a school principal would make the effort to drive to their house all the way out in the country, just to intervene on behalf of her daughter. A way was found. Grace would become an educated woman.

8. Learning to Read

There was another shooting star, and another. It was Aunt Sister Docia and Aunt Sister Gracie. Lord, how beautiful they were. The embers gathered, glowing.

Docia was the oldest of her aunts, Gracie the most sophisticated. Aunt Gracie had married and moved to Fairfield, just off the Birmingham-Bessemer Streetcar line. Her home had a fishpond and a cabinet full of pretty glass things. Grace lived with Aunt Gracie when she graduated from high school, and then got a job in Birmingham. It was Aunt Gracie who taught Grace the importance of reading.

Aunt Gracie had told her, "Honey, it doesn't matter what you read. Read those trashy romance novels if you want to. Just read something, anything. It grows your mind. With a book, you can travel anywhere."

9. Leaving the Country

She still read copiously. She had gotten two nice, thick novels as presents. She was anxious to start on them. She had gotten so many presents. So many.

She sat and stared at the embers and remembered. She allowed herself to remember *him*.

Her cousin Blanche had introduced them to one another. He was a tall, self-centered boy, very proud of his stylish hair. He worked in the Wenonah iron ore mine ... a real job ... a manly job. But he was a little too cocky, a little too full of himself, a little too needy. She would pass.

But he persisted.

They'd been married less than a year when Carroll went off to war for a while. He left her pregnant and living in his father's house. Her father-in-law was a foreman in the ore mines. They lived in a large company house in the camp. She lived with her new father-in-law, mother-in-law, their two daughters, and the mother of her mother-in-law. She cherished her new family and loved her new husband dearly. Her in-laws were supportive and treated her as their own. They were proper and hardworking, and there was even joy and laughter and affection. They were a wonderful family.

10. Big House Little House

Shooting stars. Her new father and new mother, her new sisters, as close and loving as her real kin, shooting across and gathering in the growing embers of her mind. Shooting stars. Her new father did not drift lazily across her mind. He hopped and skipped and danced across it. The star was warm and giving.

As a foreman in the ore mine, he had made good money. Soon after the war, he bought an acre of property on the busy road between downtown Powderly and Lipscomb. On weekends, he and his son built a big house out of brick, big enough so that everyone who lived in his home would have plenty of space. It had an indoor bathroom with a bathtub and a big dining room where everyone could eat at the same time. It had an upstairs with two big bedrooms. She and her husband and their two children had one of the bedrooms all to their own. Her father-in-law decorated his house very festively each Christmas. A drunk once came in the front door and ordered a beer and a hot dog. Inappropriate behavior for Christmas time, Grace had thought. The man was sent on his way, but with a Coke and a "Merry Christmas."

11. A Real Home

Frank and Ruth. She hadn't thought of them in years. Oh, how it would have been grand if they had still been alive to have come to her party tonight. But, then, they were alive, weren't they? Crossing, there, into the embers.

Living with her in-laws worked very nicely, until one day it occurred to Grace that she did not have a place of her own. The thought simply came to her. For the first time in her life, she felt real anger. She announced to her husband that she was taking their children to Mama's house. She would return when he had found them a place of their own. There was nothing further to be discussed. She left with the children. Within the week, he'd transformed the garage in the back of the big house into a beautiful, cozy cottage. It had a kitchen big enough for a table to eat on. It had a sitting room and two bedrooms. They put bunk beds in one bedroom for the children and had the other bedroom just for the two of them. For the first time in their marriage, they had a bedroom all to themselves.

Soon, the little house rang with laughter. Frank and Ruth would come over to play Canasta on Friday nights. There would be snacks, and they would tell jokes and cut up. They were never without enough food, although sometimes she *did* have to ration meatballs when they had spaghetti.

12. Home

Homer and Agnes – weren't they a trip? Both bigger than life. Homer was the wild child of the family. Ran off to join the Navy when he was sixteen. Had a tattoo on each arm. Met Agnes at a bar in Charleston. Nobody thought their marriage would last a week. They died within a month of each other. Fifty years later. Married. Their stars passed together, intertwined, bright and sparkly. They would have liked that.

Her husband bought the run-down lot adjacent to his father's house. When he had extra money, he'd buy building materials. When he had an extra hour, he would doggedly build as much house as he could with the materials that he had. He took no shortcuts. Once, he tore down an entire wall because it was a degree out of plumb. She, too, was no stranger to hard, backbreaking work. They worked together. The day came when she had a beautiful, proper home. He had copied the design from a ranch house they admired in an affluent part of town. It had a full kitchen with a separate dining room and living room. Each of the children had their own bedroom, and the parents' bedroom was away from the children's. The house had a built-in bathroom with a bathtub. The living room had a big window where they could properly decorate and display their Christmas trees. Their house was always the most decorated on the street. People were always driving by to see it. If the lights had not yet been turned on, people would stop and ring the doorbell, and ask to see the Christmas lights.

It was here they would raise their first two children, Denny and Linda.

13. Suburbia

She would move once more in her life, into suburbia. It was the only "store-bought" home in which she would ever live. They thought they would never pay off a mortgage that big. The house had a big front window, and it sat at the top of a hill. It was great for displaying big flocked Christmas trees. Their house was always the most heavily decorated in the neighborhood. Christmas was a time of rejoicing and joy. It was the time her husband was always happiest.

14. Affluence

She should really get up and go to bed now. The children would be upset with her if they knew she was staying up so late. The children's marriages had produced so many beautiful grandchildren. Each one more beautiful than the last. And all of her children had stayed married, not a divorce in her family. She was so blessed. There were so many grandchildren and great-grandchildren she sometimes had to stop to remember their names and what she had given them as presents. Each child received a present. Not as expensive as they had once been, but there were more of them, and she was not as wealthy as she had been when they owned the cleaners. How strange life was. Her husband had worked his entire life to make enough money for them to modestly live on. As soon as he retired, his friend talked him into opening his own business, a dry cleaners. Suddenly, they no longer needed to live modestly.

She managed the dry cleaners. She remembered the name of every customer, of every spouse, of every child. She suffered through their divorces, sometimes more than they. She rejoiced in their marriages. She remembered their names when they came back years later. She mourned their dead. It was not an act, not a business strategy. It was who she was. They, other than her children and family, were her life. The money came. Her husband considered himself a shrewd businessman.

She was so blessed. So very blessed.

15. Traveling

Oh, the places her husband had taken her ... to Lookout Mountain and Pigeon Forge; to Branson, Missouri; and even Hawaii and Alaska. On their 50th Anniversary, they went all the way to Cancun in Mexico with all of their children and grandchildren.

Oh, yes, and there were Beijing and Singapore and London, and Paris several times. She had really enjoyed the Holy Land, and that cruise up that river to St. Petersburg had been nice. And there were some other places, too. Had she been to Australia? She really couldn't remember. Maybe it had been Austria ... or maybe Argentina.

It was a far cry from her childhood. Living in a nice house in an upscale neighborhood with all of her successful children and grandchildren nearby. Not a divorce or a jail record among them. Oh, wait, except for maybe Mike. She wasn't sure about Mike.

She was thirty-seven when she'd had Mike. Too old to get pregnant? Ha!

16. Forever Young

Mike was everybody's best friend, but maybe a little rambunctious. He was like his Dad. Mike would be your best friend ever, or you would have to die. There was a steady flow of Mike's constantly new friends and old friends through her home. She was a second mother to them all. They kept her young. She was 37 when Mike was born. She still felt 37 when Mike married. Only then did she begin to age again.

She'd forgotten to take her pills. Linda would be furious. "Mother, you have GOT to remember to take your pills."

There went Essie and Minnie and Myrtle, Walter and Hoyt and Stella Mae. Gathering in the embers.

They had been her family. They were hard-working, caring country folk. Toward the end, Stella Mae had lost her mind. It was so horrible not to be able to remember those you love.

17. The Baby

Her first child was born in his grandfather's house in the mining camp. She loved her husband more than she had ever loved anyone, but her son belonged to her, needed her, relied on her, and gave unconditional love. Her love for the child was without end. Her son, her beautiful, beautiful baby son. She always held him close.

18. Days End

The ringing of the phone would not stop. Groggily, she answered it. "No, not yet. I was just sitting by the fire." ... "Yes, it was a wonderful day." ... "No, I'm not too tired. I was just resting my eyes." ... "Yes, I was about to get up and take my pills and go on to bed. Oh, and I know you know it, but I just want to tell you what a wonderful daughter you have always been. Everything any mother could ever want in a daughter. I love you." ... "Yes, I'm ok. Just a little tired." ... "No, of course you don't need to come back over. Everything is fine. I'm going to bed now." ... "Yes. I'll take my pills." ... "Love you."

A shooting star passed through her mind, and upon landing, segued into her father.

Her biological father had come back late in her life. Her children were almost grown. He had made a modest fortune after he had run off to Detroit. Forty years after leaving her mother, he had returned, wanting to be part of her life. What choice did she have? She loved him. He gave her a van or a boat or something really nice. He did the best he knew how.

19. What Love Is

After hanging up the phone, exhausted, she sank back into the chair.

The cold, bitter wind blew up through the cracks between the planks in the floor. She pulled the blanket tighter around her and huddled toward the dying fire. She sought her doll to hold close.

"Daddy, why did you have to leave? You could have stayed and told me stories and rocked me to sleep at night. We could have played games. I missed you, Daddy. I missed you so!

The embers did not answer. Only another shooting star ... bigger, slower ... majestic.

"Mommy, is that you? You died and had to leave me. You couldn't hold me close. You couldn't tell me I'd been a good girl. You couldn't tell me that I was pretty. You couldn't tell me that you loved me. I did the best I could, Mommy. I really did. I missed you so!"

Embers burning brightly became fire and flame. Fire and flame became the Light. Everyone was there. They were all so real, so very real. And there, standing in the center ... it couldn't be! Her heart stopped. It *was* him, tall and handsome, a little too cocky, a little too full of himself.

The light reached out to her.

On country girl feet, free at last of country girl dust, she ran down gravel roads and across fields of violets toward outstretched arms ... toward life, toward love ... and into the glorious country light.

###

NINE

EMPTY GLASS
A Midnight Conversation

by Dennis Wammack (c) 2019

What I write and why were forged on a bench near a statue by a stream in my backyard under predawn light.

My backyard is a beautiful, tiny national forest located in a suburban, middle-class subdivision with steeply wooded lots. It's an acre of hard-to-navigate land that slopes steeply to a drainage ditch I call a "wet weather creek." The creek is filled with running water except in the heat of summer. I'm not sure where it empties.

My neighbors have similar contiguous back yards, which I pretend are mine because visually they are, and only I can easily get to the creek because only I constructed a navigable pathway down the steep drop-off to get to it.

The stairway I built is constructed of landscaping timbers, pavers, concrete stepping stones, and superglue. It's a real fine example of Southern engineering. I placed a park bench at the foot of my not-up-to-code stairs. Further down, on the gentle slope midway between my bench and the creek, I placed a statue of the serene Buddha on a mossy knoll under a tree. I looked for a statue of Jesus, but they all reminded me of a British duke praying that his stock prices would go up. I went with the Buddha. I hope Jesus forgives me.

After a hard day of drinking coffee and sometimes playing bridge, if the night is beautiful, I will take a bottle of wine down to my park bench. Sometimes the creek babbles. Sometimes owls call. My wife does not drink nor like the hike to the bottom of the lot. I, therefore, drink alone. I would share my wine with the Buddha, but he doesn't drink. There was a time when I would take two wine glasses to my sitting spot in case someone joined me—one of my children, a neighbor, a relative, a drinking buddy, a friend. No one ever came.

That no one ever came was not a problem. I enjoy my own company and take counsel in my own thoughts. My problem is the words can't get out of my head because they are never verbalized.

One particular evening, I stood on my deck and looked down at my backyard. The thunderstorm had passed, and the solar-powered pathway lights were beginning to come on. There were fireflies. My wife was out of town at one of her bridge tournaments. The evening promised to be profoundly beautiful. I usually drink Merlot or Cabernet. That night, I selected a Malbec. I took the Malbec to my park bench.

Ironically, I took only one glass.

Generally, a half bottle of wine is all I drink. I feel the glow but can still converse coherently. I can handle a full bottle, but its effect is more extreme. That night, I drank the entire bottle. I finished it close to midnight. Only a few random pathway lights remained glowing. I sat planning my walk back up the long, now treacherous, stairs to my home. Warmth encompassed my body, my mind, and my soul. I glanced toward the Buddha and said, "Good night, Buddy." I rose to leave.

And then—the figure appeared—walking slowly beside the creek. A walking shadow at midnight in my backyard. I reached for the neck of the wine bottle. In the darkness, I clumsily brushed the bottle, knocking it to the ground. Without a weapon, I screwed my courage to self-confident arrogance and thought, *gut it out, little soldier, don't show fear, it's only a crazed killer.*

The shadow stopped at the end of my brick path, the Buddha between us. "Hellooo," the crazed killer called out. "I didn't mean to startle you. My topology map shows the golf course crossing to be about half a mile down this drainage ditch. If I can get that far, I won't have to trespass on other people's property. In my defense, let me say that I am far from any homes, and I hardly expected anyone to be up at this time of night, especially down by this drainage ditch."

"Wet weather creek," I corrected with feigned confidence.

"Yes," he laughed. "Down by your wet weather creek. My name is Mr. Bubb, but my friends call me Bubba, and hiking is my passion. I have probably hiked every mountain and every valley in the world. I was passing through your city and pulled into your country club. I could not resist exploring this magnificent topology. It is a beautiful area in a beautiful city."

Bubba, you don't accidentally stumble across the country club, and I seriously doubt that you happened to have an area topology map with you. I need to get the hell out of here!

"Thank you. You're very kind. I would offer you some wine, but as you saw, I accidentally knocked it over. Now, excuse me but it's late. I'd better retire for the evening."

I wondered if I dared turn my back on him. I tentatively stepped toward my stairway.

He replied, "Yes, of course. I certainly don't wish to detain you, although a glass of Malbec would have been nice."

With curiosity and a tinge of fear, I asked, "Malbec? How did you know it was a Malbec?"

"The bouquet—blackberry, plum, black cherry, a little leather, and violets, the amount of tannin. It's a clear night. The aroma carries well."

"Connoisseur?" I asked, impressed.

"Oh, yes," he laughed. "A passion of mine. All the fruit of the grape, but especially the brandies and cognacs." He paused. "I realize this to be an uncomfortable situation, but I assure you that I am no cat burglar or crazed sociopath. I am just your average, insanely rich, well-bred, highly educated gentleman who enjoys the glory of hiking at night across beautiful land. I also enjoy intelligent conversation. Will you trust me enough to share a glass of Louis XIII cognac? It's quite smooth. I won't ask to sit on your park bench with you. That would make you nervous. But you could sit on the bench, and I could sit on those glorious steps." He made no motion to come closer.

"As best I remember, I haven't said an intelligent thing since you got here. The steps are certainly not glorious, plus you would be blocking my escape route if things got weird—weirder. Bubba, you must admit things are not adding up here."

He laughed the perfect laugh. "Maybe I am a figment of imagination generated by a mellow mind. This I can neither confirm nor deny. But you don't appear to be frightened. A little concerned, perhaps. On the other hand, I suspect that you enjoy meaningful conversation, and I know you would enjoy my cognac. Make a risk-reward calculation and let me know whether you want me to leave or to stay and share my cognac."

This is ridiculous. He is not a figment of a 'mellow' mind. On the other hand, it's hard to believe that I am having a chance encounter with a nut case in my backyard at midnight.

Suddenly, I was supremely confident. I suspected that every word he had said was designed to make me so, but I was engaged. I said, "I'll sit on the steps for easy escape. You sit on the bench."

He laughed the perfect laugh.

I moved to the steps and sat down. He removed two glasses and a bottle from his backpack. He then walked past the Buddha toward the park bench and, passing me without slowing, handed me an exquisite goblet. Even in the darkness, I knew it was exquisite.

"Murano glass," he said. "From back in the day when that meant something—the finest glass in the world. Even today, no one can match it. Feel it. Fits your hand perfectly. Feels fragile, but you can't break it. Perfect weight. Perfect heft. Perfect balance. A perfect vessel for fine cognac. And now, of what shall we talk?"

"Cabbages and kings?" I offered.

"Not kings. Cabbages maybe. They're more complex." He paused, then asked, "What do you do?" as he opened a fancy bottle, extended it toward me, and filled my tumbler.

"I move sticks and moss around, pull English ivy, play a little duplicate bridge, dabble in writing short stories—that sort of thing."

"Yes," he said, filling his own glass. "I notice you are trying to establish moss around your statue of Gautama. The pleurocarpous will probably do better and spread quicker than the acrocarpous, but all mosses are divine."

"Is moss one of your passions?"

"Yes," he answered in all seriousness. He raised his glass and said, "Let us now toast to grapes, moss, and cabbages."

I raised my glass and nodded. "L'chaim."

"Are you Jewish?"

"No. But their toast is cool."

He watched me as I twirled the amber liquid, sniffed it, took an exploratory sip, held the liquid in my mouth, savored the full richness, and swallowed. He said, "The Jews have paid their dues. A most hardy tribe, still pretty much intact even after all their diasporas. A good control group, as it were." He paused. "You appreciate the Louis XIII?"

"Oh, yes. I'm no connoisseur, but I am drinking heaven's brew. Glad you dropped by and brought your cognac. What control group?"

He ignored the question. "You write, I believe you said."

"I've self-published a few short stories on a digital publishing site, but I consider myself to be a storyteller, not a writer. Writers are accomplished at their craft. I want to write well enough not to embarrass myself when I tell the little stories that ask me to tell them."

"What have you written?"

"Well, my first attempt was a gift for my oldest child. She had adopted two street dogs. They were great animals. We both wondered what their stories were before she took them in. So, I wrote their history based on the few facts we knew. It was a cute, simple, no-brainer kind of story. But it brought a smile and laughter from my daughter. Far better payment than money. Then, having written a story for my oldest, naturally, I had to write one for my youngest, this one inspired by her first rescue dog. Totally fictional, more complex, darker."

"So, your goal is to save all the dogs?"

I laughed. "There are worse goals, I suppose. But I just wanted to tell the story of two dogs whose history had been lost. Besides, I only wrote two dog stories. Then I wrote stories for my mother and mother-in-law. They were in their nineties, still going strong, but slowing down. The near-death white light phenomena have always interested me, so I took my concept of white light and wrote stories to give them something exciting to look forward to—dying."

"Say what?!"

"You would have to read the stories," I laughed. "One is straightforward and sweet; the other is more complex and surreal. But that's the extent of my writing career. I enjoyed it, but that was then, and this is now."

"Interesting. I wonder what other stories may be out there vying for your attention?"

I smiled. "I'm pretty much out of the storytelling business. I seem to have told all the stories that want me to tell them. Not enough sales, I suppose."

He laughed. "It must be tough to be a storyteller without a story to tell—as tough as being a story without a teller to tell it. I hope you find one another." He refilled our goblets. "But going back to your question about the Jews being a control group—God entered a covenant with them to maintain certain laws and rituals. If they would do these things in perpetuity, then God would ensure the long-term success of their tribe. A covenant stressed to the breaking point, I might add, when they became enthralled with the teachings of this Jesus fellow. The covenant was sorely tested."

"That's an unusual observation," I volunteered.

As we continued talking, Bubba kept the subject on religion. He appeared to be genuinely interested in my working-class, Southern Baptist upbringing. He goaded me to express my concerns with theology. I told him how I found it ridiculous to suppose that there was a gatekeeper between a person and God, or how any religion could teach its followers that their truths were the only path to God. I suggested that our myths and traditions are based on greater truths hidden by the mist of time and their retelling. I said, "I wish I knew the flesh and blood of these myths. Why are we the way we are? What happened to us?"

As the conversation progressed, and with ever more cognac, I became uncharacteristically animated. His every response, grunt, and question elicited words that I had never expressed out loud, only in conversations with myself.

At one point, Bubba said, "You are quite the chatterbox. You have strong opinions on many subjects."

I laughed, "That's because you listen, don't interrupt, and appear to care what I have to say. In real life, I don't talk that much because I don't express myself well, and I'm an introvert who never learned the art of chit-chat. That, plus most people don't care what I have to say, anyway. I'm babbling words at you because they have been trapped in my mind for so long."

"Sounds like stories wanting to be told."

"If I wrote them, no one would read them."

"What's your point?"

I shifted gears. "What about you? What stories do you have to tell?"

He looked startled but refilled our goblets. "I am the asker of questions. You are the answerer."

"That's not the answer to the question I asked. I'll try again, tell me a story worth the telling!"

He stared at me as if I were an impertinent child.

"Tell me!" I demanded.

He considered being angry but decided to laugh. "Looking for a story to tell?"

"I feel one hovering around."

He stared into his glass of cognac for a long time. "I do not volunteer my story. You specifically asked for it. The former is forbidden. The latter is permitted."

I did not speak. Is that even supposed to make sense?

He continued to stare into his glass, slowly swishing the contents. Looking up at me, he began his story.

"I was hiking through a barren land. Beside the trail sat a very young girl; beautiful, innocence personified, starving. I sat down across from her and greeted her. She looked up from her reverie, saw me smiling at her, jumped up, ran to me, put her arms around me, and hugged me. 'Big Bubba,' she said. I was taken aback. If a simple smile could elicit this reaction, then what a life of deprivation the child must be living, and what a richness of life must live within her."

'Little sister,' I asked, 'are you out searching for food?'

'No, Big Bubba. There is no food. My chief told me to leave his camp and not return.'

"Just like that. No questioning of what to do, no question of right or wrong, simply blind, unquestioning obedience. Protocol dictated that I leave her to die in peace. I hesitated. Where was that limit of my involvement, exactly? She was so innocent, so pure. Could I push the envelope? I wasn't supposed to ask, but I did, 'Don't you mind starving to death?'"

She looked puzzled. 'I don't want to starve,' she said.

'Well, if you got some food, you would not starve. Where would there be food?'

"Excuse the expression, but you could see the wheels turning in her head—a higher level of reasoning going on in that innocent mind."

She replied, 'The chief carries apples in his hunting bag. I have seen him take one from his bag when there was no food to share.'

'Ah,' I said. 'Is the hunting bag ever left unattended?' I could see the wheels continuing to spin. She was imagining the unattended bag and the food therein."

'Yes,' she replied with hesitation. 'Sometimes.'

'So, if you don't want to starve to death, what might you do?'

"I watched the wheels turn, her eyes light up, the dawn of reason, the loss of innocence, the knowledge of right and wrong ascending, the birth of higher thought processes, of higher knowledge, the weighing of good and evil. What she did with this information was up to her, but I had prompted her to think thoughts she would never have thought on her own."

"Hinted at State Secrets?" I asked.

"Much worse. I had taught her how to reason. Because her discovery was prompted, Sapiens would not develop as they should. They would not discover a fundamental truth; they would grow to interpret the charge 'dominion over the Earth' to justify exploiting Earth's resources, rather than as a covenant to protect the Earth and its creatures. My supervisor was furious. My associates had much to say, much to discuss, much to decide. I had prompted her to a level of thought that had been the responsibility of her kind to discover on their own. What actions should be taken to counteract my indiscretion? Decisions were made at the highest level, which would have dire consequences. I, of course, became a pariah, and justifiably so. There you have it. That is my story."

"*What* truth?!" I demanded.

Staring vacantly into his goblet of Louis XIII, he did not smile as he answered, "Write your stories! Set your words free!"

I studied my sad visitor then lowered my head and closed my eyes to collect my thoughts. *This is either a dream or a hallucination. It seems real enough—just too preposterous.*

Then I realized this had been a drunken conversation with a statue. *Buddha—Bubba—it was all in my mind! It wasn't real!*

Opening my eyes and raising my head, I stared for a while at the empty park bench, then glanced at the statue and smiled.

The sun rose to greet my mini paradise, and, without thinking—hungover, groggy, and lost in self-reflection—I saluted the Buddha with my almost empty glass, then savored the remaining drops of what remained. After a while, I stood and cast the empty glass into the babbling creek to be carried to I knew not where.

Then, carefully turning and grasping the handrail, I climbed my southern-engineered stairway that led to my bed.

###

THE COMPENDIUM OF REALITY

Foxie suggested I end the Anthology with a glossary of terms, specifically for the metaphysical terminology. These terms evolved over the several years the stories were written and have not remained consistent between individual stories. The Glossary concept didn't work well, so I organized the information in a more or less compendium format. The "compendium" reflects the most recent explanation's for this anthology's concepts and may not, or may, apply to the Universe in which we live.

REALITY

Established Science accepts that our perception of reality evolved from, and is limited to, our subjective experiences necessary for survival and procreation. There is general agreement that "Fundamental Reality" exists, but little agreement on what it really is. I propose these three levels of Reality.

Perceived Reality exists at the Newtonian level and is observer specific.

Transitional Reality is the interface between Perceived Reality and Fundamental Reality. Quantum Vibrating Strings interact, transform, and emerge into Perceived Realities.

Fundamental Reality exists at the Quantum level.

QUANTUM LEVEL CONCEPTS

Existing at this level are the Mathematical Construct, the extant Singularity, and the Time-Zero Planck Volumes with their content of a Vibrating String. All other phenomena and Properties emerge from this level.

The ***Mathematical Construct*** is the omnipresent, spaceless, timeless holding construct defining abstract Mathematics. It is independent of the existence of any Universe and is consistent across all Universes.

Singularity (or Seed) is an abstract concept of infinite mass with Zero Entropy. Within this Anthology, it is the concept of a Mother Universe producing a Black Hole where the mass becomes infinite, which is not allowed within the Mathematical Construct, which forces the Black Hole to become a Singularity evaporating from the Mother Universe into a non-existing space, that is, an unoccupied space in the Mathematical Construct.

__Vibrating String__ (dim String) is the fundamental component/entity/structure in the physical manifestation of existence. The totality of the Vibrating Strings is the product of a Singularity becoming resolved by dividing back into its components.

__Inextricable-Entanglement__ is the intrinsic property of the separable contents of a *Seed* being inextricably connected.

__Consciousness__ is an intrinsic property of each Vibrating String. It is the imprinted record of its state and is cumulative with each change of state.

__Collective-Consciousness__ is the sum of all Consciousness in a collection of Vibrating Strings, that is, an Entity.

__Soul__ is a label for the Collective-Consciousness of an "Entity."

Aggregate-Consciousness is the totality of all Consciousness in a Universe.

__Planck Volumes__ are the smallest volume possible in Space. Each Planck Volume in a Universe holds one Vibrating String.

__Time-i__ is the instance when an abstract Singularity interfaces with the abstract Mathematical Construct, resulting in the physical manifestation of both into a physical universe.

__Time-Zero__ is the instance of a Singularity manifesting itself from an abstract infinite mass into its smallest components of Vibrating Strings as the Abstract Mathematical Construct manifests a holding volume (Planck Volume) for each Vibrating String. This is the first instance of the property of Space.

__Gravity__ is an intrinsic attraction between Vibrating Strings created concurrently with, and as part of, the deconstruct of the Seed into its smallest components. It is the attraction of a Vibrating String to all other Strings seeking the elimination of spatial separation. At Time-Zero, there is no separation.

Space. See Time-Zero.

__Universe__ is the collective term for all Planck Volumes.

Note that at Time-Zero, all Consciousnesses are blank because no Vibrating Strings have yet interacted. Gravitational attraction is not yet in effect. Time has not yet emerged.

TRANSITIONAL LEVEL CONCEPTS

Time *i*s the emergent property of two strings between two interactions. (Between the collapse of one Wave Function and the reformation of the next Wave Function.)

Time-One is the first instance of two Vibrating Strings interacting with one another and producing an altered state. This is the first instance of the emergent property of "Time," and is the first instance of the Transitional Level.

Entanglement is the emergent property of Vibrating Strings remaining linked (Inextricably-Entangled) when spatially separated.

Experience is an Entity's history of imprinted Consciousnesses between Time-N and Time-N+1.

Note that the state of the Vibrating Strings during this Time-One is recorded by the Consciousness property of each Vibrating String. Also, this is the first occurrence of the attraction of Gravity. The relation, if any, between Gravity and Entanglement is not addressed in this Anthology.

NEWTONIAN LEVEL CONCEPTS

The following concepts and properties emerge at the Transitional Level, but the resulting manifestations are perceivable at the Newtonian Level. How these resulting manifestations are perceived is dependent on the Entity doing the perceiving, that is, an Observer.

Physics emerged from the first interaction of "Time" with "Vibrating Strings."

Chemistry emerged from interactions between "Time," "Physics," and various Vibrating Strings "Experiences."

Biology emerged from "Chemistry."

Life emerged from "Biology."

Sentient Life, within this Anthology, is synonymous with "Life" and does not require additional properties.

Awareness is an emergent property of the interaction between "Sentient Life" and Consciousness. The property allows Life to observe and respond to external forces.

Intelligence is an emergent property of Awareness interacting with Consciousness. The property allows Life to control its own actions rather than simply responding to external forces.

Reasoning is an emergent property of Intelligence interacting with Consciousness. The property allows Life to consider more than one response when controlling its actions.

Neurology is a specialized, multi-disciplined study of how "Life" with the property of "Intelligence" processes information.

Artificial Intelligence emerged from the interaction of Physics, Chemistry, and Consciousness, and with the exclusion of Biology.

Entity is any collection of Entangled Vibrating Strings that can be assigned a name at the Newtonian Level.

Observer is any Entity possessing Awareness.

ESTABLISHED SCIENCE

Established Science is science for which there is no reasonable known contradiction. Science never claims to be absolute fact and is always open to challenges to what it believes to be true. Settled Science is as close to claiming absolute fact as scientists are willing to make. Scientific theories are constantly challenged and refined.

Age of the Universe is currently estimated to be 13.8 billion years based on Cosmic Microwave Background radiation..

Universal Constants are physical quantities with an unchanging value that are constant throughout a universe and are fundamental to its structure. There are currently nineteen generally accepted Universal Constants in our Universe, but the number varies according to discipline.

Luminiferous Aether was Established Science until it wasn't. Isaac Newton first referred to Aether in 1718. The term evolved into the concept of the substance through which light propagated. The theory was not discredited until the Michelson-Morley experiment in 1887, and not totally dismissed until the acceptance of Special Relativity in the early 1900s.

Michelson and Morley, with their 1887 split-beam experiment, destroyed the concept of the supremacy of Newtonian physics and paved the way for quantum level concepts such as Einstein's relativity and Schrodinger's "matter as a wave" equation. Scientists are still grappling with the fallout from the Michelson-Morley experiment.

###

###